ᴛʜᴇ GOMORRHA➜ CONJURATIONS

by

WILLIAM MALTESE

The Borgo Press
An Imprint of Wildside Press

MMVII

FIRST EDITION

CONTENTS➜

FOR ROB➜

Who, in his capacity as editor/publisher extraordinaire, has performed more resurrections than Christ

II PETER 2:6↑

And turning the cities of Sodom and Gomorrha into ashes condemned them with an overthrow, making them an example...

THE GOMORRHA CONJURATIONS, BY WILLIAM MALTESE

INTERLUDE I➔

THE WIRE LOOP PENETRATED like a knife through warm butter. There was a whoosh of air prematurely released from human windpipe. Short fingernails clawed briefly but frantically at the slicked sliced throat and left bloody smear marks.

It was the second time Dr. Tye Winslow had killed that evening. Along with his first body, he had left chunks of his own partially digested vomit. This time had been easier. Still, he didn't look at his second victim's blood-drooling nose and mouth, death-bulged eyes, or bloody neck. He hurried into the darkness, followed by the nauseating stench of the dead man's uncontrolled release of bladder and bowel.

He was almost home—figuratively speaking.

He had done the impossible: entered and exited the Arab nuclear facility, Mahud Wadi. Getting in had been less difficult than getting out. He had been driven to the door, had been given a room for work and a bed for sleep. However, he had not been expected to leave—at least until the Arabs had their atom bomb to drop on Tel Aviv.

He was sweating despite the cold. It always surprised him how sand that was hot enough to cook an egg during the day could freeze water after dark.

He checked his wristwatch and leaned against weathered sandstone. He looked back toward the fortress.

Mahud Wadi sat on its lofty perch. Inside were palm trees, fountains, flowers. Outside were the sheer slab stones of natural cliffs.

Tye turned toward deep desert and saw the expected and appreciated two short flashes of light, one long, another short. He responded in kind, using his flashlight.

It was hard to believe it was over and that he was still alive. He was tempted to pinch himself.

"Let's have it!" Tye's contact demanded, moments later.

"Here and now?" It was a stupid question. Naturally, here and now. SODGIA would double its chances of getting the information if there were two people ferrying the data. "The Arabs are already close. I'd give them a year. They've good men. Miller from Germany. Karl Weismann from Sweden. Karl Jorge from Norway."

"They have Jorge, then? You've actually seen him?"

"They brought him in a month ago."

"Jorge could hurry things for them."

"He's not being very cooperative."

"Should he become so, and they have their ways of seeing that he does, he could shave off what? Three months? Four?"

Tye thought of mentioning the two Arabs he'd left dead in the darkness behind him. "Even if Jorge does cooperate, you should have time to come up with something, by way of a solution, shouldn't you?"

"We already have."

When the alarm bell went off, bespeaking the discovery of one of the two garroted guards, Dr. Tye Winslow was one of the scientists who exited his room in the Arab fortress and nuclear facility, Mahud Wadi, to see, it would seem, what was happening.

CHAPTER ONE➜

(I)

CHAD NORDELL ENTERED THE CAFETE-RIA, his exceptional good looks bringing their usual share of envious stares. His blond hair hung low over his forehead and feathered against his well-shaped brows. His long lashes shielded his cat-green eyes. His cupid's-bow mouth held a full and sensuous pout. All of which Carol Hilliard found irresistible, quite aside from his large trust funds, his being treasurer of Sigma Nu, his having his own car, his having a reputation of "swinging both ways", even before bisexuality became the "in" thing on campus.

He didn't join the lunch line but stood, search-ing the room. Seeing Carol, he began his weave through milling people and crowded tables that brought him to her.

"How about I steal you for about an hour?" he suggested.

Carol had hair the color of ripe wheat; it paren-thesized her pixie face with soft curls. She had blue eyes, freckles across the bridge of her nose. Her lips were neither too thin nor too thick. Wearing no brassiere, the nipples of her full breasts were clearly outlined through the expensive cashmere of her sweater. Her long and shapely legs were thigh-over-thigh beneath the table.

"Joan has a few ideas about the murder that she'd like to run by us," Chad explained.

"Sure." Carol got up and led the way until the two left behind the rush and could walk side-by-side. "Joan give any clues?"

"Something about some of us pooling our brain-power."

"You don't sound convinced."

"It does have its advantages."

Doors opened onto the University of Washington quadrangle.

It was warm for that time of year, even with the slight breeze. More than one young man was out on the grass with his shirt off, exposing summer-tanned partial nakedness to the last of the autumnal sun.

"Something about all of one's eggs in one basket," Chad added.

Carol enjoyed the feel of the warmth, and she combed her tapered fingers through her hair to provide her face with more exposure to the sunshine.

They banked left toward the row of trees on one edge of the quad.

"Multiple plans are better than one?" Carol provided the most obvious alternative.

"Yeah, maybe."

When they joined Joan Dunning, beneath the shade of a large oak, a departing Donna Hill was saying something about not knowing a Browning 35 from a Lahti M35.

(II)

GERALD TENOWSKY HAD BEEN expecting this young man and knew the proffered identification card was a fake. Ali Bahid was the enemy, merely going through the motions of attending the University of Washington, and had nothing to do with the CIA.

"When did you last see the Lows?" Ali repocketed the forged document.

Never have seen *her*," Gerald said, hooking his dirt-discolored thumb into the ring of a beer can and opening the metal top. "I haven't seen *him* since the war."

"You were friends, right?"

"I was a sergeant. He was my commanding officer. We didn't socialize."

"A *good* commanding officer?"

"One of the best. Didn't give me shit. Let me handle the men. Most every other braided monkey thought he was King of the Zoo. Not Low."

"He took over on Raunga when Colonel Wompit was killed?"

"A slant-eyed bastard shot Wompit. Low assumed command."

"The official report said 'sniper', right?"

"Damned Jap!" Gerald spat.

"You know for sure it was a Jap? I mean, you saw him?"

"Never saw or caught the bastard." Gerald opened another can of beer and waited until the white bubbles, same color as his hair, washed the can top before he took a healthy swallow. "Gook got clean away."

"Wasn't that odd? The island *was* under Allied control at the time."

"The slants were wormed into the landscape." Gerald wiped suds from his lips with the back of his right hand.

"You were assigned airport duty?"

"Had to keep our planes coming in and out, didn't we?"

"Remember the arrival of Lieutenant Colonel Randolph Miller?"

"Should I?"

"A SEDAPT flight seven days before Wompit got shot."

"Oh, *that* Miller." He slurred his words.

"How about the B-29 captained by Colonel Richard A. Stout?"

"Hush-hush shit, that one." Gerald took another long swig of his beer.

CHAPTER TWO→

(I)

HAIR WAS STANDING UP along the back of Harold Low's neck.

He stopped dead in his tracks and tried to look inconspicuous while he tried to single out who in the quad found him of such interest.

He told himself he was being paranoid. However, he couldn't shake the feeling of being spied upon.

He jumped from the hand suddenly on his shoulder.

"I've heard of absent-minded professors," Martha Low said, "but isn't forgetting one's own wife overdoing it just a bit?"

"I didn't see you."

"Obviously. Anything wrong? With your sight, or otherwise."

(II)

JOAN WORE A WHITE BLOUSE, held at the wrists by massive gold cufflinks, wide tie with blue and white polka dots; short black skirt that showed surprisingly nice legs and duplicated the color of her short-cropped hair.

Her expressive black eyes hinted intelligence.

She sat the balustrade and appeared as just one of the many students who had decided to take advantage of the sunshine. Even her continued check of her watch was explained by the sudden appearance of Carol Hilliard coming through the crowd.

"Sorry I'm late," Carol apologized. "Halloway kept us after."

Joan stood and nodded in the direction of Harold and Martha Low.

"Any set pattern, yet?" Carol asked, taking the notebook Joan handed over.

"There's always something." Joan straightened her skirt.

Professor Low and his wife passed.

Carol waited a few seconds and followed after.

(III)

AT THE SPOTLIGHT, Chad looked kiddy-corner. The lower floor contained Ange's French Cleaners, Rod's Barber Shop, Pudee-Cameron oriental Rugs. The second floor was all gymnasium, no curtains.

A fat, middle-aged man huffed and puffed around the upstairs running track.

The traffic light turned green, and Chad crossed to the other block to walk as far as Pine Street. He turned left.

It started raining. Nothing unusual for Seattle.

He put on his hard hat, printed "Kaiser Aluminum". It was a gift from a trick.

Across the street was the Westside Federal Savings Bank. The words "Imperial Theater" could still be seen through the paint on the side of the renovated building. Chad had spent many an hour of his youth with his pants unzipped in the darkness of the Imperial's second balcony.

He headed south along Fourth and arrived, finally, at the Tool Inn. He entered and passed through the restaurant area, with its busy floral motif, and into the cocktail lounge beyond.

Mark Lane, studly and with a big cock, was on duty, as cordial as ever. He gave Chad's brandy Alexander extra splashes of booze.

Chad nodded casual greeting to some of the room's patrons who were so used to seeing him they would have trouble remembering whether he had been here Friday, Saturday, or both. Most of them were already conveniently drunk.

He sipped milky froth from his glass and moved to a table.

One young man at the bar got up and put money in the jukebox. Judy Garland (how original?) began singing.

CHAPTER THREE➔

(I)

CAROL'S LAST CLASS WAS AT 3:00. She skipped it but asked Jim Winters to take notes.

She snacked at the HUB with Sally Holland, surprisingly uninterested in Sally's latest tale of Charlie Banion's twelve-inch dick and the magical things he could do with it. She was glad when Sally had to go.

She swallowed the last of her hamburger and drained her final swallow of syrupy Coke. Her stomach growled in likely preview of acid reflux probably due before her day was done.

She chewed a Tums and strolled the path to the student parking lot. She unlocked the door of her car, passenger side, and removed a piece of folded paper from the glove compartment.

The paper was Xeroxed from *Brassey's Infantry Weapons of the World*:

COLT M1911A1 PISTOL

Manufacturer: Colt's PTFA and Ithica, Remington, Springfield Armory and Union switch and Signal (United States)

19

Calibre: .45ACP
Dimensions: Length 21.8 cm / Barrel length
    12.7 cm
Weight: 1.1 kg
Effective Range: 50m
Operation: Recoil
Muzzle Velocity: 250 m/sec
Sight: Front—blade / Rear—square notch
Magazine: 7-round detachable box type

At the bottom was scrawled in pen the name and address of a Seattle gun shop.

(II)

CHAD SPIED THE FORCEPS in the glass cabinet near one wall and figured they could be useful. The cabinet was locked.

Ten minutes later, Dr. Richard Perry entered with Chad's chart.

"Got the clap again, do you?" Dr. Perry provided a disproving frown.

"I don't think so. Just thought it was time for a check-up."

"I'll send in the nurse for some blood. You can't be too careful, these days.

"So you've said before." Chad unzipped his pants.

"Have you been using condoms?" Dr. Perry took a swab from a bottle on his desk and pushed its tip into the cock's meatus that Chad obediently pouted.

"I still feel ridiculous using a rubber every time I fuck."

"You'll think it's not nearly as ridiculous if you catch AIDS while bare-backing." Dr. Perry slipped his swab into a glass vial and pushed in the rubber stopper. "Any oral or anal sex?"

"What do you think?"

Dr. Perry dutifully took additional cultures.

CHAPTER FOUR➔

(I)

JOAN STOPPED AT A GROCERY STORE for Gallo Hearty Burgundy and cheese. She purchased a fresh loaf of sour-dough bread from the bakery.

On the outskirts of town, she pulled her car to the side of the road to get her bearings. Her route was clearly marked on a map. She foresaw no problem as long as the roads were as easily found as everyone said.

She settled back into the driver's seat, slipped some Chopin into the CD player, and eased her car back into freeway traffic.

She drove for over an hour before the Jacksonville turnoff. She pulled into the right lane, accelerated, and glided the asphalt loop that curved into the countryside. At the stop sign, she turned right and pulled into the first place that allowed her to again check her map. Satisfied she was headed right, she got back on the road.

It was another rare sunny day. No one could say the weather wasn't holding.

Joan kept exactly to the speed limits.

Just when she suspected she'd passed her turnoff, she spotted it up ahead.

She turned into the first few yards of dirt roadway and braked for the thick chain hung with the warning:

PRIVATE!!!

Inside her car's glove compartment, next to her recently purchased Colt pistol, was the key that unlocked the chain's padlock.

The cabin was two miles farther.

She was expecting something rustic. There were people with substantial incomes who lived in less luxury.

It was constructed of natural timber, contained three bedrooms, two and a half baths, a dining room, living room, and a kitchen. It blended perfectly into its environment, obviously planned to do just that by some expensive architect.

Joan knew she should have expected as much, considering it was owned by Chad's parents.

She found everything waiting in the kitchen: paint-smeared newspaper spread on the floor, butcher paper rolled in one corner, used stencils off to one side, forceps on the counter next to the paint and rollers, table and chairs scooted to convert more floor into workspace.

It was eleven o'clock. Joan decided to stencil and have lunch while the paint dried.

She rolled out five yards of butcher paper on the floor and cut it, anchoring its free ends with saucers. She rolled out another strip to slightly overlap the first. She joined the two strips with Scotch tape then added a third.

She spread stencils over the paper. She covered a roller with paint first dumped into a metal tray. She imposed massive black imprints against the whiteness. She moved the stencils and made more imprints.

Finally, she put the stencils to one side and washed the roller underneath the faucet in the kitchen sink.

The paint was water soluble. Whatever had been spilled was wiped up easily with a damp rag.

Joan washed her hands and face of splatter and eyed her artwork. A lot of it was smeared, but it wasn't meant to last a lifetime.

She left her work to dry at its own leisure. She took her cheese, wine, and bread with her along the trail out back. She strolled into thick forest and emerged in a small field. She confronted a stack of sun-bleached hay bales. She noted the ground markers placed at meter intervals between her and the pile.

It was good to eat cheese and white bread. It was good to drink wine. In the end, though, she did wonder if she would be able to hit anything if she was drunk.

(II)

CHAD STOOD IN THE SHADE and looked across the asphalt at the massive cement dormitories.

It wasn't yet noon; another of those unseasonable and uncharacteristically hot Seattle days. Already, his shirt stuck to his flesh.

24

He took a notebook from his pocket and jotted down the time.

He walked the perimeter of the parking lot.

The to-rent he wanted shouldn't be too far away. It had to have at least two rooms. It had to have privacy.

He crossed the road.

It might give the plot a nice twist if the location he found was directly next door to Harold Low's; but Chad doubted that would be possible.

He walked for two more hours before finding the small vacant house that sat among high shrubs. It had a garage.

CHAPTER FIVE➔

(I)

CAROL HILLIARD POINTED THE COLT PISTOL. She sighted along its barrel and squeezed its trigger.

There was the resounding noise of firing and the jolt of recoil.

One after the other, she deliberately discharged the six remaining bullets.

Methodically, she picked up seven spent casings before going to the stack of hay.

Using forceps, she worked slugs from the bales behind the targeted black silhouettes.

(II)

"HAVEN'T SEEN YOU IN A LONG TIME," Leena West said and remained with Chad while her boss wandered with a potential customer.

The Metromere Gallery catered primarily to the tourist trade that frequented the newly renovated Pioneer Square.

"I figured it had been *too* long," Chad flattered. "Want to go to my place and fuck?"

"You know, you could almost turn me on to guys," Leena said. She had a cute, little-boy look that was miles away from stereotype, truck-driver lesbian. "You'll notice, please, the qualifying *almost*."

"It's because you always say the nicest things that I come bearing a commission." Chad knew her interest when he saw it.

Her financial situation, always precarious, had been made worse by a series of bad investments.

"What kind of commission?"

"The kind that'll clear you a hundred big ones."

"Jewelry?"

"Sculpture. Metal. I'll even supply the material: steel with traces of copper and base metals. You can easily access equipment for metal meltdown, can't you?"

"What size metal pieces are we talking?"

"Hand-sized and smaller."

"No problem, then."

"What'll it take for meltdown? Crucible? Acetylene torch?"

"I could just do it at a foundry. I've a friend…"

"I don't care what you do at a foundry, later," Chad interrupted, "but, I want to do the initial meltdown, other than in a foundry, myself."

INTERLUDE II➜

DESPITE HIS YOUTH, this was not Isaac Jo-sepheus's first mission. The Israeli Mossad would hardly have used a novice on this one.

At twenty-two, Isaac had killed more men than he had years. It wasn't that he enjoyed killing as much as he had just too often been in kill-or-be-killed situations.

He and his men checked their gear. They had done so before, but there could be no mistakes.

There was another spurt of adrenaline through-out Isaac's veins, a tautness of his muscles, and a tingling of his guts.

Suddenly, he turned toward the radio receiver and listened. The signal was short-lived.

"Ask them to confirm."

Lenard Cohen did as he was told.

They waited. Confirmation came.

There would be no Jewish assault on the Arab fortress of Mahud Wadi that night, or for many nights to come.

CHAPTER SIX➔

(I)

AT 4:36 P.M. FRIDAY, Joan checked her watch and separated from the group of students in the HUB cafeteria.

Lana Tampton saw Joan exit and called after, not once but three times; she'd wanted to borrow Thursday's humanities lab notes. She didn't pursue. She figured to see Joan on Monday; they had an econ class together.

At 4:45 p.m., Carol attended a sociology class in Wilcox Hall. She sat next to Marilyn Wilshire who noticed Carol repeatedly checking her wristwatch. Before the big hand of the college clock over the door made its spasmodic jerk to 4:46, Carol gathered up her notebook and quietly exited without explanation.

(II)

AT 5:30 P.M. HAROLD LOW dismissed his last class of the day.

He went to his office and picked up the papers he was planning to correct while at home that evening.

At 5:32 p.m., most of the students released for the weekend, Harold left Carlton Hall.

Dr. Randolph Miller stopped him at the outside fountain. The two men talked for a few minutes and went their separate ways.

At 5:47 p.m., Harold was home and depositing his briefcase in his den.

At 6:00 p.m., he began his evening walk.

Sarah Wesley, preparing supper, looked out of her kitchen window to see Harold take the pathway into the small ravine.

(III)

MARTHA LOW CHECKED HER WATCH and called Sarah Wesley.

"I just saw Harold out for his evening constitutional," Sarah said. "I wish I could get Nathan to do the same. He's getting a middle-age spread."

"I've an errand for Matthew if he's up to it. I'll gladly give him a little something for the few minutes it'll take him."

"I'll send him right over." Sarah laughed. "He has a date, later, and his father, as usual, is being stingy with cash."

It was 6:30 when Mat Wesley rang the Low doorbell. Martha noticed the time because, among other things, her grandfather clock chimed the half hour.

Matt was seventeen, with an athletic build and blond hair. He was dressed in a suit which made him look awkward. The knot of his tie was lowered over the opened top button of his shirt, revealing a *V* of smooth and hairless athletic flesh.

"Just drop this off at Tillson's for me, will, you Matt?" Martha reached into her apron pocket and removed a film chip. Tell them to run off a couple four-by-sixes of each for pick up tomorrow.

She gave Matt more than enough money to make it worth his while.

(IV)

AT 7:15, CAROL ENTERED THE ROOM.

Chad was taking off a protective mask.

As soon as he left, Carol walked to the crucible on its makeshift stand of insulating bricks. She opened her purse and took out a Colt pistol and a paper sack filled with bullet slugs and casings. She placed the bag and the gun next to the crucible and proceeded to don the protective gear Chad had just vacated. Once shielded, she dropped the automatic, and the sack, slugs and casings, into the crucible.

Carefully, she removed the blowtorch from its holder and aimed its jet of ignited gas directly onto the crucible contents.

The copper was the first to run, going liquid beneath a spouting of sparks.

By the time Joan entered the room, it was impossible to tell what Carol and Chad had dropped into the melting pot.

Joan, Colt pistol out, fished her coat pocket for bullet slugs and casings, melted them down, and then went to join Carol and Chad in the other room.

(V)

AT 7:30, MARTHA CALLED DR. RANDOLPH MILLER.
I thought Harold might be there," she said.

"I haven't seen him," Randolph answered. "I just got in from supervising a lab-test. Anything wrong."

"I hope not."

Martha hung up and called Sarah Wesley.

"He's not here, hon," Sarah said. "You getting worried that your absent-minded professor has forgotten his way home?"

Nathan Wesley said something in the background.

"Nathan is putting on his coat, Martha. He'll go down the ravine and take a look-see."

(VI)

AT 7:45, NATHAN FOUND HAROLD. He called Martha, telling her to come over as quickly as possible, but only after he'd called the police.

(VII)

"THAT'S ABSURD!" SARAH INTERRUPTED.
"What is?" Inspector John Linehan asked.

"What you're insinuating."

"Which is what?"

"That Martha might have killed her husband."

"I've insinuated no such thing."

"Well," Sarah said, turning her attention on her friend, "don't answer anything, hon, until you see your lawyer."

"It's all right," Martha said.

"Mrs. Low?" John said, then repeated.

"What was that?" Martha finally responded.

"Where were you at the time of the murder?"

"What time was that?"

"About six-thirty."

"I was home."

"By yourself."

"Who else would be there?" Sarah injected.

John gave Sarah a glance that sent her into the kitchen for fresh coffee.

"Did you see or talk to anyone?" John asked Martha.

"Mat was over for a few minutes."

"Mat"

"My son." Sarah said from the kitchen. "He ran a film chip to the print shop for her."

"What time was that?"

"About six-thirty," Martha and Sarah said in unison.

The telephone rang; Sarah answered it.

It was Randolph Miller calling for Martha: "Martha? I thought you might have contacted the Wesleys about Harold."

"Harold is dead, Randolph."

CHAPTER SEVEN→

(I)

"DO YOU KNOW A STUDENT, here at the university, named Alan Wayne?" Inspector John Linehan asked.

"I beg your pardon?" Martha sounded on-guard.

"I know this might be an embarrassing subject for you, Mrs. Low, and I wouldn't be asking if it didn't have possible bearing on your husband's murder."

"You can't possibly suspect Alan!"

"We'd just like to ask him a few questions."

"I see." Martha sat on the sofa. She gazed out the front window. "And just what exactly is it that you'd like to know?"

(II)

"WOULD YOU LIKE TO START at the beginning?" John asked.

"How many times does this make?" Joan asked. There was the faintest trace of a smile on her lips. "You must have heard this a dozen times, just from me alone."

"You do realize this isn't a game, Miss Dunning? We're talking a murder. Premeditated and cold-blooded."

"Then, might I suggest you head on out in search of a premeditating, cold-blooded murderer?"

"You don't think that's what I'm doing here?"

"You're taking undue advantage of an unfortunate coincidence."

"You find it mere coincidence that Professor Low was shot to death in the exact spot picked by three of his students for a class project? You find it mere coincidence those students each destroyed a pistol, one of which was possibly the murder weapon?"

"We were simulating certain aspects of a *theoretical* crime, Inspector. We were *not* participating in one."

"Would you like to take it from the top, again—please?"

"From when Professor Low divided his Abnormal Psychology class into two segments, you mean?"

"He instructed half of you to plan perfect crimes, the other half to solve them?"

"He always does that. Ask anyone. The whole point being that he didn't believe there was such a thing as a perfect crime."

"Three of you decided to pool your talents."

"Yes."

"Whose idea was that?"

"I'm not sure."

"Surely, it wasn't a simultaneous decision."

"Maybe it was. Three brains are obviously better than one."

35

"Did *you* suggest it?"

"It resulted from a mutual gab-session."

"*It* being your plot to kill Professor Low."

"It could as well have been a plot to kill you. It just seemed fun to let the old fart grade us on his own murder."

"Whose idea to use a gun?"

"It was, again, a group decision. The gun was chosen, because, of the overpass; shots could be mistaken for backfires. Or, maybe the ravine was picked because of the gun. No one sat around keeping those kinds of notes."

"If no one kept notes, how did you remember what was decided?"

"There are notes, and there are *notes*. We might write down the location selected but not who suggested it in the first place."

"You're sure you can't tell me who first suggested the ravine or the gun?"

"Ours was a think tank, Inspector. If one of us thought we had a good idea, or something to add, we'd just spit it out and let the others have at it."

"Tell me about the ravine."

"We took turns watching Low. Like most everyone, he has...*had*...a degree of regimentation in his life. We merely needed to isolate those certain times in his schedule that were most opportune for his murder. The ravine was an obvious location choice. It was isolated, easily accessible; it had the highway overpass. Low went there every night."

(III)

"I'D LIKE TO LET THE LAB TAKE A LOOK AT THIS," John said. His fingers tapped the head of the metal miniature.

"Suit yourself." Chad shrugged.

They were in Chad's apartment, within walking distance of the campus.

"Do you know it's against the law to destroy a weapon used in a crime?"

"Is it?" Chad poured himself a refill of Chevas Regal. He had offered John one, but his offer had been turned down.

"Yet, you proceeded to melt down three pistols and convert them into this bit of metal sculpture?"

"While it may be against the law to destroy a weapon used in a crime, is there any law saying someone can't melt down personal property? I assure you, Inspector, not one of the melted pistols was utilized for anything other than target practice.

"You'll swear to that?"

"Bring on the stack of *Bibles*. As I said— Between five-thirty and nine o'clock, on the evening in question, I was with Carol and Joan. I swear. As all of us had our guns at that time, none of those weapons could possibly have been off killing Low. Cross my heart."

"But weren't the three of you *supposed* to choose separate hiding places, during the time of your lesson-planned killing?"

Chad sat on the couch; John remained standing.

"Ours was a plan, Inspector, which was never intended for complete implementation. So, there was no real need to draw blind lots to determine which of us would do the killing. There was no need for each of us to rely upon the other two to lie for us."

"So, why exactly did you so thoroughly carry out only *some* parts, like buying weapons, target practice, locating a murder site, observing the daily routine of Professor Low, and melting down the guns?"

"We were unsure about being able legally to obtain the guns, about becoming proficient in their use, about melting them down in finale. If we followed through on those, no one in the solve-the-crimes other half of our class could logically refute those things could be done. However, anyone can find a private place to hide for a couple of hours, can't they? Who's going to successfully argue the impossibility of that?"

"I'll tell you what I think. One of you got carried away and moved beyond mere conjecture, because all of you went through each and every aspect of your plan for murder, including isolated concealment. Two of you now sit scared shitless, because you don't have real alibis but did have a gun and a working knowledge of how to use it. These two are relying upon this fabricated meeting of the three of you, from five until nine, to protect their asses. In the process, the killer ends up undetected."

"Excuse me if *I* think your theory comes across just a tad too Agatha Christie."

Chad's glass was again empty. Rather than refill it, he turned the crystal to clink remnant ice cubes.

"What about motive?" he asked finally.

"I've seen people kill for far less than the thrill of being part of a perfect crime."

"Ah, yes, the Leopold-Loeb Syndrome."

John eyed Chad closely in an attempt to fathom something other than the handsome young man's indignant innocence.

"It might interest you to know," John said, without a clue as to what Chad was thinking, "that the late Professor Low and I are of like mind on there being no such thing as a perfect crime."

(IV)

CAROL'S SORORITY SISTERS—despite their curiosity —vacated the lounge area.

"You're not concerned that you may be concealing the killer?" John asked.

"Christ, yes, I'm concerned!" Carol disagreed. She sat down on the piano bench and looked at her hands. She was beginning to bite her nails. She hadn't done that since the onset of puberty.

"Let me tell you what I'm trying to do," John said quietly. "I'm trying to eliminate suspects. The way it stands, you three have given each other an alibi. But if you weren't with the others, but still had an alibi, I would be better convinced of your innocence."

"Jesus," Carol moaned.

"There must be something," the Inspector persisted. "If you went to a movie, maybe you have the ticket stub. Something else, anything else, placing you away from the scene of the murder at the time of the murder."

"From the beginning, we realized it could fall apart at this point," Carol said. "So, we made sure we played by our rules."

"Maybe we can decide your innocence another way, then," John suggested.

"What other way?"

"Maybe you forgot to destroy all the bullet casings or slugs from your pistol. All we need is one to compare with the ballistics report on the slug that killed the professor."

"There were no leftover slugs or casings. They were all gathered up, methodically counted, melted down."

"I find it hard to believe you did everything so thoroughly. I find it harder to believe that you didn't each plan for some way to verify your innocence in case something went wrong."

"There was no reason we should have taken precautions to assure our innocence. As far as we were concerned, there wasn't going to be a murder. We were carrying out mere hypothesis. Following the rules made it more fun and interesting. We did so easily, naturally, precisely, because we didn't have something in the back of our minds telling us it was for real. It was something which merely *could* be done, not which *would* be done."

She stood. It was a nervous reaction. She sat again.

"Let me tell you something I learned from Professor Low," she said. "A real criminal can be subject to pangs of genuine guilt, because he usually has an inherent sense of right from wrong. He can be tripped by his subconscious into feeling a need to be caught. That's why no crime is perfect when dealing with a human and all the guilt-ridden foibles that come with being human. In this case, however, you're dealing with two—probably three—people who had no guilt, because they knew from the get-go there would be no crime. There were no inner voices telling us we were wrong, no subconscious mechanisms strewing clues this way and that so we would be caught and punished. The crime was conceived, in the majority, by innocent people who planned and executed so well because their interest was in the mechanics of successful means and not in the actual execution of an inconceivable end. If one of us *is* guilty, and I don't really believe that for a moment, what percentage of our plan was the killer's and what percentage that of the guiltless other two? If one of us is guilty, don't look for too many clues, because I very much doubt there going to be there for you to find."

"No matter how much of the plan was conceived in innocence, the guilty had his—or her—finger in the pie," John reminded. "Often one clue is all we need, and even the cleverest criminal will often leave us one."

"And if none of us is guilty. If you're barking up entirely the wrong tree?"

CHAPTER EIGHT➜

(I)

"YOU MUST BE OUT OF YOUR MIND!" Martha Low stated, the shock of Alan Wayne's unorthodox arrival still in effect. Being awakened with someone's hand pressed tightly over her mouth wasn't anything she would find welcome under any circumstances.

"Quiet, goddamn it!" Alan commanded. "I think the cops have a plant outside."

"Sure as hell they do," Martha verified. "They expect you to come waltzing in here. That's a helluva lot more than I ever thought you'd be stupid enough to do. This bravura of yours is liable to put your neck in a noose."

"Just how much *do* the police know?"

"They know we were meeting. They know what gossips want to make of our meeting. That, if nothing else, gives them reason to suspect you had a hand in murdering my husband."

Alan sat on the edge of the bed. He was in the same clothes he wore when he left the dormitory supposedly to meet Chad Nordell for sex in the Arboretum; Chad hadn't showed.

"I didn't do it, you know," he said with finality.

"Of course you didn't do it."

"I was in my dorm room with a friend. "I heard about Harold's murder on the eight-o'clock news."

"You'd better come up with a lie better than that. The police have someone who says you left your dorm with plenty of time to commit the murder."

"Damn!"

"Where in the hell *did* you go?"

"I went for a walk. Can you imagine? Sounds like something out of the plot of a B-grade movie, but that doesn't make it any less the truth."

CHAPTER NINE➔

(I)

"WHY THESE RED CHECKS?" John's index finger moved down the left-hand side of the notebook page.

"Things Professor Low did daily," Chad said.

"This large *X*?"

"His walk through the ravine."

"Who physically put this *X* on this page?"

"You want to put the handcuffs on me now?"

"*You* made these other marks, too?"

"For Christ's sake, Inspector. At one time or another, all three of us had our hands on that notebook. How in the hell am I supposed to remember who made each and every hen scratch?"

"But you do remember making this *X* for the spot of the murder?"

"Yes."

"When?"

"When the ravine was definitely decided upon as the murder site, I guess."

"On a Friday? Saturday? Sunday?"

"Never on a Sunday."

"Was it two days before the murder? Three days? Four?"

"I haven't a clue."

"Who first decided on the ravine? You, Dunning? Hilliard?"

"We *all* decided, or haven't you been listening? Not that anyone, spending five minutes examining Low's daily routine, wouldn't have seen the ravine's obvious advantages as the spot for his murder."

(II)

"PROFESSOR MILLER AND MY HUSBAND were in the war together," Martha said and poured herself a cup of tea. "On some Pacific island."

"They kept in contact after the war?"

"They didn't become friends until meeting here, Inspector. They didn't even remember meeting during the war until they, one day, began comparing war stories over cocktails."

"You don't remember the name of the island?"

"I'm afraid not. All of those islands have such weird names, don't they? I probably wouldn't even recognize it if you said it and got it right."

"Would you say your husband and you were close to Dr. Miller?"

"Close? How do you mean?"

"Did you do things together? Did you go over to his place? Did he come here often?"

"Yes, to all of those, although Randolph *is* something of a loner. The rest of the faculty only see him at occasional get-togethers. He'd probably skip those, too, if Dean Rochester wasn't so insistent the faculty interact."

"Did your husband and Miller often get together professionally?"

"It wouldn't have been unusual. Randolph's field of expertise is psychiatry. Harold was always interested in Randolph's opinions, insights, and input."

"At the time of his murder, do you know if your husband was conferring with Dr. Miller on anything?"

"Harold hadn't confided in me for years, Inspector. That's probably why I turned to Alan Wayne."

"Your husband knew about Wayne, then?"

"I don't know *for sure* he knew, but the chances are more than good that he did, yes—and didn't give a damn."

(III)

JOHN FOUND PROFESSOR RANDOLPH MILLER AT HOME.

Randolph, just under six feet, showed evidence of a once good physique. He was smoking a pipe when he answered the door, the smell of cherrywood tobacco heavy in the air. He seemed genuinely surprised when John identified himself, but he recovered sufficiently to invite the Inspector in and offer him a chair.

"You're here about Harold, of course," Randolph said. It wasn't a question.

"You've been expecting me, surely," John said.

"No matter how much one prepares for this sort of thing, one never really succeeds. May I offer you a drink?"

"No, thank you."

Randolph sat opposite and took a puff on his pipe.

"Mrs. Low says that you and her husband served together during World War Two."

"Hardly *together*." He rekindled the failing flame in his tobacco. He waited until the pungent weed was again smoldering before he continued. "We were once, briefly on the same island. It was one of those sheer coincidences that makes for interesting parlor conversation years later."

"This was in the Pacific Theater?"

"Raunga. Harold was permanently stationed there. I was passing through for assignment to SEDAPT."

"SEDAPT?"

"Security Division, Armed Forces, Pacific Theater."

"You and Low never recalled meeting there until he became a professor here at the university, is that right?"

"Actually, he was teaching here when I arrived."

"You became friends?"

"I think you can say that."

"You saw him frequently during the work day?"

"As large as this campus is, it was actually possible for us *not* to see each other for virtually weeks on end."

"Then, you had little communication with him prior to his murder?"

"We had a few brief encounters." His teeth firmly anchored the stem of his pipe.

"How many meet-ups would you consider *a few*?"

Randolph shrugged.

"What if it had been suggested that you went out of your way to meet with Low on several different occasions, just prior to his murder?"

"I'd say you'd been speaking with someone who likes to exaggerate."

John took the notebook from his pocket and put it on the coffee table. "Do you know what this is?"

He flipped open the cover and ran his finger down one page of notations. He stopped at one.

"Eight o'clock: Low talked briefly with Dr. Miller."

He flipped the page and pointed to yet another entry.

"Low met Dr. Miller at the HUB, and they went to the faculty area."

"As I recall it, Harold was convinced the Wayne boy was *out to get him.*"

"Alan Wayne? Out to get him, how?"

"Harold refused to give Martha a divorce."

INTERLUDE III➔

RAMILE MOHAMMED'S FACE, arms, and legs were burnished chestnut by the sun. His chest and belly, back and buttocks, were a paler brown by comparison. Naked, he looked like some freakish hybrid, older than his thirty-eight years. He certainly *felt* older.

He slipped on his shorts and shirt and sat on the edge of his bed to pull on his sweat socks and boots.

This morning, he would again search the desert around Mahud Wadi. Another radio signal had been picked up. As usual, it had been of short duration. It might have been mistaken for static if Ramile didn't know otherwise in his infinite wisdom. Somehow, he just knew it was connected to those two mysteriously garroted guards.

He finished dressing for another day on the sand. Each day was a battle with nature. This wilderness area had swallowed his brother and father without a trace. He had no doubts that it could, and probably would, one day swallow him as well.

CHAPTER TEN➔

(I)

JOHN GLANCED AT THE REPORT that had arrived that morning by private courier. It had an accompanying letter from Brigadier General Norman Frank.

The report contained the war record of Lt. Col. Randolph Miller, and it was impressive.

Randolph had enlisted one month after the U.S. entry into WWII. He had received a direct commission after six months of active duty in the European War Zone. He had been wounded twice and apparently still had pieces of shrapnel in his lower back. He had led an assault on a German machine-gun nest, knocked it out and killed ten of the enemy before downed by a leg wound. He was awarded the Medal of Honor *for conspicuous gallantry and intrepidity at the risk of life, above and beyond the call of duty.* He received two Purple Hearts. By the time of his honorable discharge, he had an impressive list of decorations which included the Distinguished Service Cross, the Distinguished Service Medal, the Bronze Star with clusters....

His arrival on Raunga in 1945 was in conjunction with his transfer to the Security Division of the

Armed Forces in the Pacific Theater. As he told the Inspector, and as General Frank verified, the details of his assignment were still under wraps, all of these years later. However, the General had known Lt. Col. Miller personally, both during and after the war, and could vouch for the man's integrity as an officer and as a gentleman. The General also stated that since all SEDAPT operations would soon be declassified, he thought it within his authority to mention that nothing in any of them would indicate anything but an indirect connection between SEDAPT's Raunga operation and Colonel Harold Low.

All very nice. However, John took all such reports with a grain of salt. His own experience had shown military brass not averse to stretching the truth when the purpose suited.

John's length of service with the police force had, likewise, convinced him that a military background did not necessarily insure truth or straight and narrow. Not to mention the several people John had put behind bars that had used their military training in pursuits that were less than honorary. More than one Medal of Honor winner had failed to keep his killer instincts exclusively confined to the battlefield.

CHAPTER ELEVEN➜

(I)

MARTHA WAS SPRAWLED UNGLAMOROUSLY on bloodied sheets. She had a second mouth at her neck where there shouldn't have been one.

Sarah Wesley and she had been scheduled for morning coffee. Martha hadn't showed, and Sarah had been concerned when her friend didn't answer phone or doorbell.

A cordon of police formed outside the house to block curious onlookers. Bad news traveled fast.

"Anything?" John asked one of the lab men inside.

"Well, the murderer seems to have washed in the bathroom sink. Cheeky! Hopefully, I'll be able to tell more later. Then again, maybe not."

"Christ, what a way to go!" John breathed heavily and doubted he'd ever be able to look on a dead body as just one more inanimate object in a roomful of inanimate objects.

(II)

RANDOLPH MILLER'S SURPRISE looked real enough.

"You hadn't heard, then?" John asked.

"Christ, how could I?"

"It's all over the campus. All the media has the story by now."

"Martha, Martha." Randolph stepped back and looked every bit a man in shock.

"You were saying that you hadn't heard?"

"I've been under the weather." He went to a bottle of liquor on a small silver tray and half filled a glass without bothering to ask if the inspector would like to join him. He took a big gulp and made a face as the booze went down.

"Nothing serious I hope."

Serious?"

"You not being at school."

"A slight fever. I've had recurring bouts for years, since the Pacific."

"You haven't listened to the radio or television?"

"Splitting headache." He sat down and took another gulp. "Who killed poor Martha?"

"You?"

"You think *I* killed her?" His follow-up laugh was hollow and devoid of humor. "Kill her? Christ, I loved her!"

"Want to run that by me one more time?" Obviously, John was sure he couldn't have heard correctly.

"I loved her."

"I would have been very interested to hear that before now."

"I suppose you would, if just to use it as a motive for my possibly murdering Harold. Except, I have an alibi to clear me of anything to do with Harold's death, don't I?" He was conducting a make-up lab and hadn't left the classroom.

"It certainly seems that you do. It, also, seems that you and Mrs. Low kept your affair *very* low profile."

"It wasn't easy to do, I assure you."

"What about Alan Wayne and Mrs. Low?"

"Martha wanted a divorce, and we decided it would be easier to get one if Harold discovered she was having an affair with one of his students, instead of with me. It wasn't difficult for her to seduce the horny Wayne kid. He'd fuck, and had, anything in a skirt—or a pair of pants. Harold, though, it turned out, didn't care. He expected Martha to have affairs. She was considerably younger than he was, you understand."

"So, you and Martha, arranged to have Harold killed?"

"I have my alibi. Martha had hers; something to do with the neighbor kid."

"If Wayne had learned of the hypothetical murder planned by three of Harold Low's students, he might have passed that on to Martha in pillow talk. Whereby, you and Martha could have hired someone to meet Low in that ravine."

"Hit men readily available to university faculty, are they?"

John shrugged.

"What did Wayne think of your affair with Mrs. Low?" That was something John certainly wanted to know.

"He didn't have a clue."

"How did you and Mrs. Low manage that?"

"Love is blind?"

Did Randolph realize that he'd just given Wayne a motive for Martha's murder? What if the kid found out he was being used as a pawn in Martha's divorce, destined to be replaced soon enough by another man? "Let's get back to you at the time of Mrs. Low's murder."

"I was in bed. Alone."

"A shame; the *alone* part I mean."

"I loved her, damn it!"

(III)

THAT MARTHA LOW AND RANDOLPH MILLER had selected the Random Heights Hotel for their supposed romantic interludes bespoke a professionalism that John Linehan found disquieting. Two amateurs, first-time involved in an adulterous relationship, didn't usually pick a place as big or as popular. The stereotype motel for such things—out of the way and seedy—*was* the usual reality. The reasoning seemed to be that things were best hidden in such less-frequented places; it was one of the commonest misconceptions held by the adulterous segment the population.

In fact, those in search of ambiguity were ill-served by small motels.

Whatever the photograph flashed before any seedy manager, it was likely he, bored as he was, could recall the who, when, and where.

On the other hand, so many people frequented a big hotel that it was usually impossible for the hotel personnel to recognize individual names or faces, especially of any two people who weren't regulars.

"They *were* here, Inspector," the Random Heights's desk clerk surprised. He hadn't recognized their names or their photographs—neither had anyone else on the staff, for that matter—but he had been cooperative and looked through back registration files. "They checked in on that Monday afternoon and left the following Tuesday morning."

"Will you check a couple more of those names and dates," John requested.

"I can go only back six months. Anything before that will be in the basement."

"Check what you can, then."

John was curious as to how quickly Randolph had come up with exact pseudonyms and exact dates. As good as Martha might have been in the sack, she couldn't have been so consistently terrific as to make each and every time with her indelibly imprinted upon her lover's memory.

"Here's another one." The clerk handed over the second registration card.

John compared signatures likely made by one and the same person.

"What are these numbers?"

"Room number, rate, check in date, estimated time of departure."

"And this *T* after the room number?"

"Twin."

"You mean *two* beds?"

(IV)

"**I DON'T KNOW, JOHN,**" the voice emerged from the telephone earpiece. "They're always extremely sensitive about queries incoming from *any* quarter."

"Ernie, you know I wouldn't ask if it weren't important."

"That wouldn't be Central Intelligence Agency, by the way. SEDAPT was absorbed by SODGIA after the war."

"SODGIA?"

"Security Office, Division of Governmental International Affairs."

"You have someone inside, Ernie?"

"We don't make it a habit to infiltrate sister security organizations. Even if we did, it's damned hard to get us to admit it."

"This *is* important, my friend."

"Listen, John, if you've got something ongoing that involves SODGIA, bale now and save yourself the deluge of red tape."

"I'm not even sure SODGIA is involved. I'm just trying to find out."

"And the guy's name, again?"

"Randolph Miller. Lieutenant Colonel at discharge. Excellent war record. Transferred to SEDAPT after duty in the European Theater."

"Just what is it you want to know, John?"

"*Anything*, Ernie."

"I can't make any promises."

"Have I ever asked for any?"

Pause.

"And, could you check on Martha Low while you're at it? Not with SEDAPT, because she wouldn't have been old enough at the time. Maybe some connection with SODGIA."

CHAPTER TWELVE➔

(I)

"BUT WHY?" JOHN ASKED, perplexed to the point of anger.

"It's a promotion for Christ's sake!" Hammond Williams said and tried to contain his own anger in having been put in this situation.

"None of it is a wrap, yet."

"So? Leave the wrap to Whittaker."

"Just leave me on for a few more weeks. I've things in the works that may crack this wide open."

"You're referring, I suppose, to your recent queries to a certain governmental agency as regards Randolph Miller and Martha Low? Jesus, John, how could you have been so damned stupid?"

"*That*'s why you're relieving me?"

"Let's not get carried away by paranoia. You've been seeing too many spy movies. No one really tells anyone else to keep their fingers out of the proverbial pie. You're being removed, pure and simple, because you've earned a little rest and relaxation *and* a promotion; all of which you will, by the way, advantage, no more questions asked."

(II)

"YOU BETTER SIT DOWN," Jack Borack said and put his briefcase on the desk; Patrick Fowler stood at the window across from him. "You're definitely not going to like what I have to tell you."

"I had that impression from the moment you appeared at my door." Patrick went to his desk and sat.

"Martha Low is a possible wet-job."

"Whose? Certainly, not ours." His voice was controlled but he'd been trained to keep it that way.

"It just may be that the Wayne kid is Israeli Mossad."

"Jesus fucking Christ!"

(III)

HENRY GLOPSTEIN'S BUSINESS was money. It used to be clothing: Glopstein's Clothing Emporium. That store still stood, filled with merchandise. Customers still bought there. Cash registers still jingled; money still changed hands. *That* ching-a-ling, however, was now chicken feed. Henry was into bigger things, having raised literally millions for Zion.

He had started fundraising on his own, walking up and down streets to squeeze dollars from fellow Jews who had already given to the professional fund raisers who constantly bemoaned Israel's scant chances for survival without the financial backing of *World* Jewism. He had been so successful in squeezing blood out of the proverbial beet that his true potential was quickly recognized by the powers that be.

Now, he was the best money-man on the West Coast. He was known for successfully coaxing cash from wealthy Jews who, like anyone else, found it hard to associate with the poor and/or the struggling masses, even of their own faith.

His prime targets often had problems associating with their inner Jewism. Their personal Zions were mansions, pools, private schools for their kids, and country clubs for themselves. Their philosophy was that hard-earned cash was better off buying another Cadillac than another M4 Super Sherman tank.

He motioned for Alan Wayne to begin.

"During World War II," Alan addressed his well-heeled audience, "there were, it would seem, initially three atom bombs, not two, scheduled to be dropped by the Americans on Japan; one of which turned up missing. An offer was recently made to sell that long-assumed-lost bomb to the Arabs. Your help and your money are needed to make sure this doesn't happen."

INTERLUDE IV➔

THE SUPPLY OFFICER FOR THE ARAB barracks at Daladin was surprised when Ramile Mohammed personally showed up. He couldn't believe a few cans of missing tinned meat were worth his superior's time and attention. Within any large organization, there was internal theft and/or things that just fell through the cracks. Such occurrences were so regular, there was an accounting entry specifically designed just for them.

What he didn't know was that Ramile Mohammed was convinced the thefts had not been made by soldiers for extra cash on the black market but by Jews broadcasting illusive radio messages. Even Jewish pigs had to eat; and Ramile was positive they didn't have a supply line extending all of the way back to Israel.

He never, for one minute, doubted what those crazy bastards were doing out there, holed up like rats in a part of the desert from which even the rats had been expelled years ago.

CHAPTER THIRTEEN➔

(I)

CLARENCE HENLIN BEGAN, mainly speaking to the new faces in the room.

"Code name: Project Gomorrha has the primary objective of destroying the Arab nuclear research facility presently existing at Mahud Wadi.

"It has as its secondary objective underlining, for the world, once and for all, those dangers inherent in allowing nuclear capability to fall into the incompetent hands of *any* smaller, volatile nation or group.

"The plan is designed to make it appear as if Mahud Wadi's destruction is caused by a malfunction of an atomic bomb under development on-site. This is to be achieved by introducing an atomic bomb with special detonation devise to be activated by our mole already placed within the facility.

"The bomb for sale is being passed off as one of *supposedly three* assembled under U.S. supervision on the Tinian Island group in the Marianas in 1945 for dropping on Japan.

"Our three sleeper agents, acting as sellers, were Professor Harold Low, Martha Low (nee Hemming), and Dr. Randolph Miller; all residing in and around the University of Washington, Seattle, Washington state, Harold Low and Randolph Miller on staff.

"Both men were conveniently together, albeit briefly, on the Pacific island of Raunga during World War II. Raunga one of several islands originally considered and then rejected for basing the B-29 bombers that carried the Nagasaki-Hiroshima payloads.

"Another contributing factor was Low and Miller on Raunga when a B-29, commanded by Colonel Richard A. Stout, took off from the island on 2 August 1945, flying a routine mission, forced to ditch at sea, no survivors.

"All of which has been used in our cover story that convinced the Arabs that Low and Miller, while on Raunga, sabotaged the Stout B-29 flight in order to cover up the fact that the third a-bomb which should have been on board wasn't, having been previously hijacked by Low and Miller.

"Miller's premature recall from Raunga supposedly left Low in sole charge of the bomb's final disposition. Low, whose reason for stealing the bomb was always supposedly altruistic, had reason to keep that location from Miller whose motives have been portrayed as purely mercenary.

"All of these years later, our story cover goes, Miller, still seeing the hijacked bomb as a cash cow, enlisted the help of Martha Hemming to charm the secret of the bomb's whereabouts from Low, Martha becoming so intent upon her mission that she went so far as to marry Low to ferret out his secret.

"Martha supposedly found out the location of the bomb from her husband, passed on that information to Miller who passed it on to the Arabs.

"Now, however, Harold *and* Martha have possibly been murdered by an Israeli operative, Alan Wayne. And the Arab buyer, Ali Bahid, once posing as a student at the University of Washington, has dropped out of site.

"Ideally, we'll pick up the Arab involvement, again, when and if they move to pick up the merchandise.

"What we have to brainstorm, here and now, is how we minimize additional interference, from the Jews and/or from anyone else.

"Any questions?"

(II)

DR. TYE WINSLOW HAD A HEADACHE. He also felt sick to his stomach.

He lie quietly, eyes shut, and tried to gather his thoughts. All of that was difficult to do.

His ears picked up sounds definitely *not* indicative of his daily routine at Mahud Wadi.

A door opened. Footsteps. A painfully bright light greeted the slow opening of Tye's bloodshot eyes.

"Ah, Dr. Winslow," Ali Bahid's not ungentle hand went to Tye's forehead. "I'm glad to see you're coming around."

"Where am I?" Tye wondered how many times, in how many B-movies, that hackneyed question had been asked.

"Let's just say that you're a good many miles away from Mahud Wadi. I should think this little jaunt would be a welcome change of pace for you."

The blinding light that kept Tye from properly focusing came through a circular window across the room from him. Motes of dust floated within the spotlight-like glare. They were swept into a maelstrom of movement when Tye wiped the back of one hand across his weary brow.

"Your mental and physical feeling of fuzziness will wear off in a couple more minutes," Ali assured.

"I feel drugged?"

"Maybe that's because you *have* been drugged. It seemed to be the best way to quietly facilitate your exit from the fortress."

"But why?" Tye was paranoid, especially at the thought of having been injected with some sophisticated truth serum that may have already sucked his mind dry.

"No need for you to be needlessly concerned," Ali said. "You're merely on a mission of extreme delicacy where your special knowledge will be extremely useful."

Tye struggled to a sitting position. His vision cleared somewhat. His nausea remained.

"This is a boat?" he asked. That would account for the rocking, for the porthole, for the other-than-drug-induced sick feeling in the pit of his belly. He never had managed all that well on water.

"Actually, I think the vessel is officially large enough to be called a *ship*."

Tye was there for several reasons. One, he was an American. The Americans had been mainly responsible for those first nuclear bombs. It was assumed an American would be familiar with design and operation. Even at this late date, it was necessary to protect against fraud. Then, there was the chance the bomb was real but weathered to the point of *too hot to handle*. There were few qualified Arab nationals who could be unobtrusively loaded on a ship and sent to the Pacific. The world, frightened into an awareness of big bombs suddenly possible for small nations, had eyes constantly focused for just such possibilities. Since Tye was incommunicado at Mahud Wadi, it was easier to move him than one of the Arab nuclear physicists whose appearance in the Pacific would set off major bells. Besides, Tye was sympathetic to the Arab cause.

"Just relax and consider this a little vacation in the sun," Ali suggested. "Once the drug wears off, make your way topside. It's actually a very beautiful day outside."

CHAPTER FOURTEEN➔

(I)

KILLING A PERSON WAS LIGHT-YEARS BETTER than killing a horse, and a million times better than killing a dog, and far-far better than killing a cat.

Killing Martha Low had been better than killing her husband.

In killing Martha, Chad hadn't even had to manhandle his stiff dick to achieve orgasm— spontaneous ejaculation had occurred, as surprisingly nice as it was unexpected.

Then again, he always knew killing another human being would be good. SODGIA's insinuation that he'd soon enough be doing *just that,* transformed into another James Bond with license to kill, had been his sole reason in letting the agency recruit him on the college campus in the first place. All these months later, though, it having become all too obvious that SODGIA had reneged on its part of the bargain, Chad had felt it necessary to take matters into his own hands.

If he'd waited for SODGIA to tap his full potential, he would still be continuing his boring university existence, a mere gopher (go-for) in a game plan that kept him on the periphery while Martha and Harold Low and Randolph Miller had all of the goddamned fun as major players.

Certainly SODGIA hadn't asked or expected Chad to kill Harold and Martha. In fact, SODGIA would be downright perturbed if and when it ever found out that Chad—not Alan Wayne who had turned out to be an Israeli operative, and who would have guessed that?—had done the deed. Chad had chosen Alan as the fall guy for Martha's murder entirely because Alan had been conveniently fucking the woman and had wanted so desperately to fuck Chad. That the horny Alan Wayne turned out to be a Mossad spook, screwed royally (figuratively if not literally) *by Chad*, was ironic justice that proclaimed Chad a genius at doing what he was doing.

Soon SODGIA would realize that most of its original good-guy players were out of the picture *but Chad*. If not, Chad would have to kill someone else (Randolph Miller?) to get the agency's attention.

Now that he had killed twice, Chad had no intention of *ever* stopping.

(II)

HE PARKED HIS CAR and turned out its lights. Across the street was a warehouse-like building that seemed dark and deserted. In front of the building was a line of motorcycles. A door opened somewhere within the darkness and spilled light and the tinny sounds of cowboy music out into the street.

Two men exited the bar. Both were in leather, the blackness of the night making them shadows within shadows. One of them went to a Honda 1050 GEX and mounted it. His muscular thighs gripped the highly polished machine as he started it up. His companion crawled on behind. In a minute, the motorcycle and riders were roaring down the street.

Chad got out of his car, locked the door, and crossed to the bar. He had been here several times. He found the butchness of the Rusty Cell more enjoyable than the tamer gay haunts he'd preferred once upon a time.

He put his hand to the door and pushed.

He nodded to the leather-clad bouncer who sat the stool just inside.

His entrance was accompanied by the usual interested and disinterested stares.

He paid little attention but went to the bar and ordered a Bud. In a masturbatory grasp, he carried his cold bottle with him into the shadows adjoining the pool table.

"Out for a little action?" someone asked.

Chad kept his attention on the two shirtless guys playing pool. One player dropped the nine ball in a side pocket.

Chad turned briefly to the kid beside him who had white-blond hair cut in a buzz-cut. He had an excellent body poured into tight-fitting jeans and a black T-shirt.

Chad sipped his beer and didn't bother to answer.

He turned his attention back to the game in progress.

One player hunched over the green felt, his bulged crotch evident and hinting of *his* balls even bigger than those on the table.

Chad scoped the whole room, in no hurry.

It didn't take long for him to realize, though, that the best potential for his evening was the kid still standing right beside him.

"Are you new in town?" Chad said finally. He thought he'd seen the kid before. Not likely seen him in here, though. So many of the people in the room were interested in the kid, it was obvious Chad was dealing with new meat.

"Nah," Chuck Daller answered. "Just new to this bar. I usually hang out at the Tool Inn."

CHAPTER FIFTEEN➜

(I)

"I THINK YOU'D BETTER SEE THIS," Jeff Marcheus's lead-in came off ominous.

Clarence Henlin grimaced. Bad news wasn't made better by delay. He took the offered file folder and opened it on his desk.

"The bodies have been identified?" He tried to focus impartially on the grisly pictures.

"Arabs *and* Jews. The last picture, by the way, is the one you'll certainly not want to miss."

Henlin shuffled the colored deck.

"Jesus! Is that Dr. Tye Winslow?"

"Apparently, he was brought out of Mahud Wadi to confirm the bomb in the field."

"And did he activate any or all of the timing mechanism?"

"We don't know whether or not he did, or whether or not it was the Arabs or the Jews who won the battle so obviously fought for the bomb."

"Jesus H. Christ Almighty!"

(II)

THE *PERUVIA* WENT DOWN stern first. Ali Bahid watched from the only lifeboat to survive the sinking.

The Arab comrades Ali had just killed were expendable, all locked in one of the ship cabins so they wouldn't float to the top. It was simply unfeasible to risk letting them be captured.

He rowed toward the breakwater. Shadowy palm trees dotted the awaiting landscape.

Water slamming shallow-growing coral got louder and louder.

Ali stopped rowing and let the current suck him nearer an open channel.

He stripped off his clothes and stuffed them into a large plastic bag. He filled the remaining bag space with air and tied off the open end.

He took the ax brought from the *Peruvia* and hacked a hole in the deck of the lifeboat.

Ten minutes later, using the plastic bag as a float, he reached shore; the boat didn't.

INTERLUDE V➔

RAMILE MOHAMMED WAS NOT the only Arab interested in the sporadic radio signals exiting and entering the territory around Mahud Wadi.

Bara Raziz was six feet of compact muscle. He had dark black hair that shone with the grease worked daily into its strands.

He had a face that could be called surprisingly attractive in spite of its puckering scar that ran from his right eye to his mouth. He had performed the mutilation himself, knowing few men would think him anything but a pretty plaything had he continued to look as girlish as he once had.

Raziz had been far luckier than Mohammed in discovering the illusive source of the radio signals. His men had not only located Isaac Josepheus's band of Jewish swine but had killed all but two of them in a genuinely genius sneak attack.

He did not inform Ramile Mohammed of his success. Raziz, after all, was as much a fugitive from Mahud Wadi security forces as was Josepheus and his little band. Ramile represented the government in power: official landholders. Raziz, on the other hand, represented a displaced Arab nation, homeless. He was Palestinian, his parents driven from their rightful lands by Jewish dogs. He had never been in Palestine, having been born after the flight from Jewish atrocities, but his father had told him of the land that was rightfully theirs. Bara Raziz had promised, at his father's deathbed, to regain what had been stolen from them.

It was an interesting paradox: Raziz not only at war with all Jews but at war with many of his brothers in Islam. When Palestine had been usurped by invading Jews, a whole Arab nation had been forced to flee into other Arab countries. Arab hosts, still holding land and determined not to share it, looked upon Palestinian refugees and guerrilla activities as a threat to their own tenuous relationship with Israel. While any Arab leader risked political suicide by turning overtly against the Palestinians, there was unofficial censorship which made Raziz and others like him resentful.

The guerrilla forces had power by sheer number. They were a nation of displaced persons. And that nation multiplied in the wilderness. Despite thousands of babies who died in the refugee camps, there were those who survived the hardships of birth. Early struggles for survival conditioned them for the greater battles yet to come. After having lived in the squalor, the hunger, the clouds of flies and human filth, a refugee had really very little to fear when fighting for something better.

The Palestinian guerrillas were interested in the activities at Mahud Wadi. While the Arab League saw the facilities as their upper hand in future dealings with Israel, the guerrillas saw them as something more. The Arab League might use any atomic breakthrough to bargain for a return of certain parcels of conquered lands, but the guerrillas believed the Arab League had lost all interest in insisting upon the reestablishment of an Arab Palestine.

The Americans wanted an Arab-recognized Israel. The Russians seemed content with the status quo, recurring problems with the Chinese making them wary of any unnecessary involvement. Europeans, as usual, didn't give a damn about anyone but Europeans.

Raziz had no qualms about what any nuclear bombs manufactured at Mahud Wadi could and should be used for. Palestinians couldn't lose anything more than they had already lost—except their lives. And they didn't fear death. Their inherent religious beliefs, bolstered by centuries of battling *The Infidel*, assured them the sword was the easiest way into Paradise—easier even than constant prayer or fasting. Raziz would rather parts of Palestine perish in a cloud of radioactive dust than be made eternally unclean under the heels of circumcised Jewish pigs.

He brought the two captured Jews with him into the deep desert, away from Ramile's patrols. Here, amid a large outcropping of sandstone, he made camp. There were no trees, barely enough grass for the camels. The water, deep in a lone hole, was brackish and disturbingly medicinal in taste.

Raziz's prisoners were in poor condition. However, he was little concerned with their health. What *did* concern him were their reasons for being in the area around Mahud Wadi and the meanings of those messages which had been sent and received on the radio now in Raziz's custody.

He had Josepheus stripped naked.

There was fierceness to Josepheus's struggles, even though the man was obviously exhausted, starved, and dehydrated, that made Raziz suspect prolonged torture would be necessary to make the Jew talk. Since Raziz had available to him none of the accoutrements for sophisticated interrogation, he had to count upon what he *did* have available to make the two Jew captives talk.

Raziz had Lenard Cohen brought to him.

"I'm going to show you what *you* can expect," Raziz said and sounded as if all of what was to happen was as painful for him as it would be for Josepheus and Cohen.

There was a boulder leaned against a cliff-like jutting of sandstone. Two Arabs clambered on top of the rock and braced their backs to the cliff. Josepheus was dragged to the boulder, his front smashed against it, his arms lifted to those men on top.

With his body held from above, each of his legs was grasped by an Arab from below. The result was his spread-eagling in a standing position, his belly, chest, and cock pressed tightly into the hardness of the stone.

Another Arab arrived. Raziz greeted him, noticing Cohen's eyes fastened on the newcomer's massive physical bulk.

"Jew, this is Gramal," Raziz favored the giant with an affectionate pat on the back.

Gramal grinned amiably. His eyes registered child-like curiosity.

"Gramal is a big help to all of us," Raziz said. "We only occasionally have the opportunity to reward him." He turned to the Arab and pointed to Josepheus's skinny ass half covered in shadow. "We've brought you a little present, Gramal."

Gramal's smile widened over teeth in various stages of decay.

"See how excited Gramal is?" Raziz observed to Cohen. "He, in his child-like way, doesn't see anything wrong with Jewish ass. That's why we delegate certain duties, concerning it, to him."

Cohen's eyes grew wide, his pupils lost within their whites.

"You think you might have misunderstood what I just insinuated?" Raziz asked. "I think not."

Again, Raziz turned to Gramal. His hand moved from where it rested on the giant's back and pressed forward against Gramal's massive chest.

Gramal was dressed in brown khakis, the chevrons of a corporal sewn with huge and uneven stitches on one sleeve. His armpits were drenched with sweat. A massive trail of perspiration ran from his bull-like neck to his waist, and Raziz's fingers followed that trail of dampness to the man's unbelted trousers.

It was evident Gramal was becoming sexually aroused.

"My friendly giant, why don't we show our Jewish friends how much Allah has compensated you for your arrested mental development?"

Gramal looked confused, but Raziz made his instructions a simpler and more easily understood, "Strip!"

Gramal's thick and callused fingers fumbled to unbutton his fly, his grin widening as he noticed Cohen's expression upon seeing what Gramal had been instructed to show him.

Josepheus screamed at the viciousness of the ensuing assault, his chest, belly, and cock going bloody as it was ground by the fucking giant into the supporting stone.

Cohen tried to turn away, but Raziz wouldn't let him and even threatened to cut off Cohen's eyelids. At the end of which, Raziz asked if Cohen too, would like to be split on Allah's avenging sword.

CHAPTER SIXTEEN→

(I)

"EUREKA!" JEFF MARCHEUS PRO-CLAIMED, entering the room and handing Clarence Henlin the photograph. "Look who resurfaced."

"Ali Bahid," Henlin said, identifying one of two people in the photo.

"It came in on a routine identity check from Honolulu. The man on his right is Shamil Marhuat. He's in oil. With a name like that, what else would he be in, right? He's suspected of funneling high-grade intelligence to the Middle East."

"How did Bahid get to Hawaii?"

"We only know he didn't arrive via commercial transport, unless he came in under an alias and successfully ducked all security cameras."

"Certainly, it would be nice to have him give us some answers."

Marcheus awaited instructions.

"You go to Honolulu," Henlin said finally. "I want someone I can trust to coordinate activities on that end. In the meantime, I'll see what I can do about bringing Chad Nordell up to speed. The fact that Bahid and he attended a couple of classes together may prove helpful."

"You really think we *can* get Nordell up to speed? So far, his involvement has been purely sideline"

"All I think is that he's the best we've got, under the circumstances. We'd certainly have less chance of convincing Bahid a meet-up with Dr. Randolph Miller was coincidental."

(II)

THE SOS FROM THE *PERUVIA* said it was sinking five-hundred miles south of Tahiti. The distress signal was picked up by an oil tanker with Scandinavian registry.

The tanker was part of a fleet owned by Sjorn Shipping, a subsidiary of Denmark Trade, controlled by Middle East oil money in general and by Shamil Marhuat in particular.

The *Peruvia* had been nowhere near Tahiti when it went down.

(III)

"I'VE NEVER SAID TWO WORDS TO THIS GUY," Chad said and tossed the photograph of Ali Bahid to the coffee table of the room assigned him at the Royal Hawaiian. Simultaneously, he was delighted SOGDIA was finally coming around as far as his potential. Better late than never. Granted, it had taken his hitting his superiors over their heads to get them to sit up and take notice—but, hey, it wasn't as if he hadn't enjoyed sending Harold and Martha Low to *never-never land.*

"We're hoping you can improvise," Jeff Marcheus said and wondered if he was handing over to this green kid more than Chad could chew. "We know you're new, but it's easier for us to get you up to speed than to bring in someone who really doesn't have a clue."

"You mean you'd like me to go, *'Hi, Ali. You probably don't remember me, but I used to admire your exotic dark looks from afar on campus and fantasize getting in your pants. No time like the present to make that a reality'*?"

"Whatever it takes. Although be forewarned, nothing we've dug up insinuates he's gay. You'd probably have more luck with his brother, Riad."

"You want me to kill him?"

"We want you to see if you can't find out whether he has the bomb and, if he does, where it is."

(iv)

THE RE WAS DEFINITELY SOMETHING about routine that made a man comfortable. Although the dead Howard Low would verify, if he *could* verify, the obvious disadvantages.

It was the disadvantage of Ali Bahid's routine (at least to Ali) that he regularly swam early-morning pool-lengths behind Shamil Marhuat's Hawaiian mansion.

The bazooka-launched rocket took out the mansion's front gate while Ali was exiting the water.

The towel in the pool boy's hand was replaced by a Colt M1911A1.

Ali figured he was a goner until the boy turned the gun butt-forward and handed it over.

Ali wasn't surprised it was a mere boy who came to his assistance. Converts were getting younger and younger.

"This way," the boy instructed.

Ali followed. There was gunfire from the front of the house.

The boy went to his hands and knees through a hole in a hedge. Ali followed quickly, his face literally against the youth's retreating ass.

Ali had cased the place on his arrival and had mapped all potential escape routes, but the kid seemed to know where he was going and what he was doing.

"Over that stone wall." The boy pointed. "We head down the beach to the left. There's supposed to be one of our men posted along the way, but I wouldn't count on his still being able to lend a hand."

Explosions vibrated the ground beneath them.

"The property ends by those double palms." The boy again pointed. "I'll go first. If there are problems, get out however you can."

He moved fast. A few minutes later, he stopped, low to the beach. He motioned Ali to follow.

Less than a minute later, they reached the awaiting car.

The kid drove the dirt road adjoining the beach. Finally, he turned onto the asphalt of a main artery. He continually checked the rearview mirror.

The car reached the heavy traffic that slowed in front of tourist-crowded hotels.

"Put your gun in the glove compartment," the boy instructed.

"I feel safer with it where it is."

"Maybe, but you'll be conspicuous as hell on the beach with it."

"What makes you think I'm going to be on the beach any time soon?"

"I have to try and find out what happened back at the house. I can't risk taking you with me. Since you're dressed for the beach, you'll blend right in."

The car pulled to the curb. Reluctantly, Ali slipped the gun into the glove compartment.

"I'll be back, right here, at five o'clock this evening," the kid said. "If I'm not, you're on your own."

Ali opened the door and felt vulnerable as hell, especially only wearing his Speedos.

The car edged back into traffic.

(v)

"I DO BELIEVE I SPY AN OLD FRIEND of yours," Jeff Marcheus said. "Why don't you go say hello?"

"The things one does for God and country," Chad said and brushed sand from his swimsuit. The next thing he said was to Ali: "Goddamn, small world!"

Ali's expression was all, *What the…?*

"Chad Nordell. You're Ali Bahid, right? We're at university together."

Ali's mind immediately placed Nordell as one of the kids suspected in the Harold Low murder.

"Are you here for quarter break, too?" Chad asked.

"Right." Ali was glad for that excuse, since he was hard-pressed for another.

"Finding much action?"

"A little." Ali assumed Chad wasn't talking gunshots.

"Where are you staying?"

"With friends."

"How about a drink at my place? I've had about all of the sun I can take for one morning."

"Sure." The idea of holing up in a hotel room for a few hours had to be preferable to getting sunburned out in the wide open.

CHAPTER SEVENTEEN→

(I)

THE PROBLEM WAS THAT Dr. Tye Winslow was no longer at Mahud Wadi. Dr. Tye Winslow was dead on some South Pacific beach. And Dr. Tye Winslow was who was supposed to activate the Trojan Horse a-bomb once it was delivered, if it was delivered, through the gates of Mahud Wadi.

An obvious alternative was to abort. Somehow get the bomb back from Ali Bahid, if Ali Bahid even had it.

Why had Clarence Henlin never seriously considered those options? Because there was simply too much time, too much money, too much planning, and too much effort already invested in this operation to bring it to an unsatisfactory conclusion now.

There was no question in Henlin's mind, one way or the other, that the original objective *had* to be achieved.

(II)

ALI CAME AWAKE SUDDENLY, rising from his chair to his feet so fast that he got dizzy and disoriented. His heart beat so hard and so fast that it seemed ready to burst his ribcage.

"Are you all right, guy?" Chad was in the bed across from him.

Ali's sleep-dilated pupils finally focused.

"I'm fine," he insisted.

Except, he wasn't fine. That had to be obvious even to this fucking innocent in the room with him.

What in the hell *had* Chad thought when Ali, gone after they'd had a few drinks, had so quickly returned when it became obvious the pool boy had failed to make rendezvous on the beach?

Chad hadn't blinked an eye at Ali's cockamamie story of a roommate caught mid-fuck and begging Ali to disappear for the evening without even a change of clothes.

"You'd be more comfortable in bed with me," Chad invited, for not the first time.

"The chair's fine, really." Ali sat back in it. "Really."

Even if Shamil Marhuat were still alive, how could Ali expect to make contact? Phones would be bugged. Houses and offices would be watched.

"Did you kill Low," Ali asked

"Me?" Chad laughed.

Ali leaned back. "So who did?"

"My guess would be Alan Wayne. He was fucking the professor's wife, right? He wanted her to himself, and her husband was in the way. Speaking of fucking, are you sure you wouldn't like to fuck me, here and now?"

(III)

"ARE YOU RICH, THEN?" ALI ASKED. *Rich* could be helpful. He was thinking better now that some of the tension had been drained from him with the frantic spurts of his cum blasted, all night long, up Chad's tight asshole.

It was morning.

Chad was on the lanai, soaking up morning sunshine.

"Certainly not as *rich as an Arab*." Chad's sunglasses hid his eyes while mirroring Ali's nearly naked body. He fantasized how it would be to kill Ali and fuck him until Ali's corpse went as stiff as Chad's dick. "A few more hikes in oil prices, and my trust funds will be completely drained just by my buying gas for my car."

Ali smiled uneasily. He got up and walked to the balcony's metal handrail. If he leaned out and looked left, he could almost see Shamil Marhuat's bombed mansion beyond the palm-sheathed flanks of Diamond Head.

"Actually, I have plenty of money," Ali said. "I'm simply having trouble accessing it."

"This isn't your version of, *'Dear Mr. Nordell. I'm an African princess, and the Nigerian government has tied up my two-billions which I'd be more than willing to split with you if you could only provide me with the mere two-thousand dollars I need for legal fees'*?"

How much simpler it would be for Chad if he didn't have to play the innocent and ask such stupid-ass questions. However, the possibility of his any other way going with Ali, on the latter's ensuing wild ride, wasn't damned likely.

CHAPTER EIGHTEEN➜

(I)

"THINK YOU'LL HAVE ANY TROUBLE filling Mr. Bahid's shopping list?" Chad asked.

"I shouldn't think so." Jeff Marcheus looked up only after he'd finished reading the items in question. "There's nothing here that a spoiled rich boy like you shouldn't be able to get, even without my assistance. Has your new fuck-buddy given you any indication where the bomb is?"

"He's said very little, aside from his sexual moaning and groaning, except that he's a CIA agent in trouble. Although I would suspect his wanting a yacht rental, complete with winch and scuba gear speaks volumes."

Jeff thought so, too.

CHAPTER NINETEEN→

(I)

"DEFINITE ARMS BUILD-UPS HERE, here, here, and here." Alan Wayne's rubber-tipped pointer stuck the map where Jewish borders adjoined Arab territory.

"And how many recent Arab raids?" Meyer Bregrael, head of Israeli's Institute of Intelligence and Special Assignments (Mossad), asked his only nephew.

"Surprisingly few. There *was* a skirmish at Janislian with no casualties. Hit and run. Little organization."

"You smell something major lurking, though?"

"Yes."

Meyer provided a loud sigh. He hadn't slept much lately. His eyes were baggy, his whites gone to pale egg-yolks. He'd been drinking way too much. "No sign of the American a-bomb resurfacing, except for the possibility related activities in and around Garuna?"

"Garuna could be a diversion," Alan suggested.

"I don't think it's a coincidence that it's so convenient to Mahud Wadi."

91

"It's going to be as difficult as hell for us to get a group in undetected."

"Maybe we need only send in one."

"Does anyone, here, really think our people already on-site are physically and/or mentally fit to handle an intercept?"

"We Jews have always been a durable people," Meyer said.

"What if the Arabs have them, the continuing radio signals just to fool us?" It was something Alan had been thinking for a very long time.

"There have been no detectable deviations from normal transmission procedures."

"The Arabs can be quite persuasive."

"I know Isaac Josepheus," Meyer said. "He'd die before consorting with the enemy."

"And Lenard Cohen?" Alan had read Cohen's psyche report.

"They're *all* Mossad, yes?" That didn't convince Meyer, either. That said, there were so few options.

"Even with a successful insertion, what about extraction?"

"I don't think anyone, especially you and I, any longer thinks extraction is possible."

"I'll go in, then," Alan said.

When Meyer's sister, Alan's mother, found out, she'd never forgive her brother or her son—even if their efforts had saved Israel.

CHAPTER TWENTY→

(I)

"WELL?" BARA RAZIZ ASKED.

"They're sending someone in," Lenard said. He'd passed the point of rationalizing himself the coward he was. He'd simply succumbed to the threat of meeting the same fate as Isaac Josepheus: ass raped, cock and balls sliced off, skin peeled, and guts poured steaming onto hot desert sand.

"Why send in someone now?" Raziz's question wasn't so much to Lenard as to himself.

It was always a question of *why*. Why had the originally planned Israeli assault on Mahud Wadi been called off? Why had the Jews kept their men at the ready? Why was someone being sent in now?

Did any or all of it have anything to do with the build-up of Arab fortifications ongoing at Garuna and Mahud Wadi?

"They only said he was on the way and supplied rendezvous coordinates."

Lenard wasn't dispensable quite yet.

Raziz left the tent. The camp had to be moved immediately.

The chances were good that the security forces of Mahud Wadi or elsewhere had, likewise, picked

THE GOMORRHA CONJURATIONS, BY WILLIAM MALTESE

up the latest Israeli transmission. If no one at Mahud Wadi was as knowledgeable as Lenard Cohen, they might still pinpoint the receiver.

CHAPTER TWENTY-ONE➔

(I)

RAMILE MOHAMMED APPEARED the more European. He, after all, was neatly fitted in pressed shorts and short-sleeved shirt.

His companion wore the traditional black robe and dark-cloth *keffiyeh*.

However, Ramile had never been outside of Arab territories. Riad Bahid, on the other hand, had traveled extensively and been educated abroad. Perhaps it was his long exposure to other cultures which returned him, now, full circle, to adopt so many once-jettisoned-by-him Arab "things".

Riad, at forty-four, stood just less than six feet. He had a slender but muscular build. His skin was an attractive bronze. His strikingly blue eyes (courtesy of a French legionnaire in the family genealogical woodpile), were shielded by thick, sooty lashes, and arched brows.

He was related by blood to Bedouin sheiks, two of his uncles on the Arab Political Advisory Council (APAC). His brother, Ali, was a prime participant in the ongoing process to acquire an antique American a-bomb.

What had the bastard Jews done to Riad's brother, Ali? Possibly, even more importantly, where in the hell was the American a-bomb?

Riad was in charge of Mahud Wadi. He was chosen not so much because of his scientific background (next to none), but because he had an inherent predisposition for administration.

"I've read your reports." His tone was less superior-to-subordinate than equal-to-equal. "I've brought you in from the field to clarify, if possible, certain aspects of them."

"Of course, sir." Ramile used "sir", because he didn't know what form of address to use. Riad's control over everyone and everything in and around Mahud Wadi was absolute. If Riad made mistakes, he was accountable only to himself and to the High Command.

In the old days, there were proper salutations. In the old days, Ramile would have prostrated himself, his eyes to the ground as he spoke. He was nostalgic for those old days. The Arab rush into the modern world left vacuums as many customs and traditions were hastily jettisoned with nothing to replace them.

"You've reported continued short radio-blast transmissions to and from certain sectors, which you believe to be Jewish in origin," Riad said. "Now, there has been this latest broadcast of longer duration."

"Three days ago, sir."

"Longer but still too short-lived to isolate any exact point of reception?"

"Correct, sir."

"But you found a recently abandoned campsite?"

"It *appears* recent, yes, sir." In a desert, traces could survive for literally centuries or be wiped clean in an instant.

"You believe the last incoming transmission was received by a radio at this one-time camp."

"Yes, sir."

"But in seeming contradiction, you think the campsite was Palestinian. Do you infer, then, that Palestinians got to the Jews before you did?"

"Possibly they did." Certainly that *could* have happened.

Palestinians were the new nomads of the desert. Deprived of homeland, they had to live somewhere. The High Command instructed peaceful coexistence between land-owning Arabs and Palestinians on the move. Palestinians were usually allowed to come and go as they pleased, with one exception.

Twice, the security forces around Mahud Wadi had fired on Palestinian bands violating the hundred-kilometer off-limits radius.

"This abandoned camp is within the prohibited zone," Riad said.

"Yes, sir."

It could mean nothing. Palestinians were like children, tempted by the forbidden.

Then, again, it could mean a helluva lot. It never paid to underestimate the potential of danger of anyone or anything.

A problem, of course, was that the Palestinians had been continually shat upon and had grown tired of walking in the offal. They blamed the Jews and whomever else, fellow Arabs included, who had agreed, however tacitly, to the reapportionment of Palestine without concern for the Arabs who had

97

lived there for generations. More and more, they grew tired of what they saw as apathy on the part of their brothers in Islam.

Arabs with pieces of territory still to lose too often sat back with a certain degree of indifference, whether feigned or not.

Palestinians were increasingly indignant that the Arabs who could didn't fully utilize the power of oil-embargo to bring the Americans "around", but they didn't have a clue how close the U.S. had come toward, and still threatened to *take* all the oil they wanted, without any asking.

(II)

LENARD COHEN WAS COLD. It wasn't entirely the chill of the desert after dark, although that was certainly a part of it.

As instructed, he'd given the prescribed signal with his flashlight. He'd received reply.

Now, he waited.

He took a mental survey of himself and knew he certainly looked the part of someone marooned behind enemy lines for days on end. His clothes were in shreds. He was dirty. His hair, everywhere, was matted and a nesting place for vermin.

He heard a sound and aimed his Beretta M51 in that direction. His pistol and its lone live bullet were but props Raziz had provided.

"Alan Wayne materialized from the darkness.

"Welcome," Lenard said with a hint of sarcasm. "Cohen here."

"Well, Cohen." Alan crouched among the rocks to keep a low profile. "I was expecting Isaac Josepheus."

"You're about five days too late. You're almost too late for *any* of us."'

"What happened to Josepheus?" It worried Alan that Cohen looked *so* bad. Then, again, what had he expected? It was miracle enough that Cohen, or any of the others, survived, period.

"Dead. What else? Killed by the Arabs who, by the way, know we're here. All of us afraid that, even in spite of that, we'll somehow be expected to try and take Mahud Wadi at this late date."

"Could you have once taken it?"

"Sure. Blown our trumpets and had the walls come tumbling down. Now, though, we've misplaced our trumpets. Have you brought us replacements?"

"You are all still members of the elite Mossad," Alan reminded.

"Right."

"And, I will get you out of here."

"Are they sending in a plane, then?"

"How long it'll take for exit will depend upon how long it takes us to accomplish our revised objective."

"If you've come with any revised objective other than getting us out of here, you're wasting your time."

"As a loyal member of the Mossad, you *will* follow instructions. If you are told to go into hell, you *will* go there!"

"You mean, I'm not *there,* already?"

"Listen to me, Cohen, and this is very important. Do you think, after all you've been through, that you would now be asked to do something if it weren't necessary for the salvation of all Jews?"

If only Alan were dealing with Isaac Josepheus. Having known Isaac in the kibbutz, Alan knew he could have been counted upon him to summon up whatever the necessary reserve required of him and his men.

"The Arabs have bought themselves an a-bomb," Alan said. He had to say it, sooner or later. It was better to tell Cohen now and let him be an indicator of how the others would react to the news.

"Why would they buy one when they're making one at Mahud Wadi?" Lenard was sweating. His throat was dry.

"As a back-up and/or to keep anyone else from getting it. A bird in the hand is worth two in the bush. Except that we—you, I, and the rest of us, here—are going to take that bomb from them."

"Dream on."

Not what Alan wanted to hear.

"Then, we—you, I, and the rest of us, here—are going to defuse the weapon and make it inoperable."

"Before or after this hell we're all in freezes over?"

"I don't like or appreciate your negative attitude, Cohen. You *do* have some notion of what the Arabs will do with an a-bomb, purchased or home-made, once they have possession of it?"

Oh, Lenard knew, all right. It didn't take genius IQ to figure it out. He also had it figured out that there was no stopping the inevitable. If the Arabs at Mahud Wadi didn't do it, then Bara Raziz and his guerrillas would do it. This little charade between Lenard and this newly-arrived fresh-as-a-daisy gung-ho piece of officer shit was a useless exercise in futility. It was already written that neither Lenard Cohen nor Alan Wayne would live to see the end— whatever the end.

Lenard stuck the barrel of his Beretta M51 in his mouth and discharged its one live bullet.

CHAPTER TWENTY-TWO➔

(I)

THE SEA WAS GLASSY except for the wake made by the rented yacht's bow slicing through.

The sun was warm.

Chad stood at the railing and watched the passing coastline.

Land had come into view two days before, but Garuna was still over the horizon.

Chad had chosen to become an agent for the sexual excitement, and another hard-on told him he wasn't disappointed.

(II)

BARA RAZIZ WAS NOT PLEASED. He had misread Lenard Cohen, and that disturbed him more than he cared to admit.

More disturbing was Raziz's realization that Alan Wayne was going to be a far tougher nut to crack than Cohen was.

Raziz should never have allowed Cohen even one live bullet, even if it would have looked suspicious if Wayne had noticed the gun was empty.

What were the odds in favor of Wayne having ever had a clue? So much for superfluous detail!

Raziz ate goat stew for his midday meal. He drank thick, black coffee from a small cup. Finished, he went to the tent being used for Alan Wayne's interrogation.

Alan was conscious, bound to the center tent pole, naked.

He had no illusions. He was a dead man, even though he still breathed. He was too familiar with the Arabs to hope he would be set free. His mission now had no possible way of successful completion. That had become obvious the moment Cohen's brains splattered desert rock and splashed Alan, even before the Arabs swarmed out of the darkness, like Army ants, to confirm the writing on the wall.

Still, though the game would go to the Arabs, Alan hopefully still had a few surprises left. Oh, there was no possible way anything he did would affect the eventual conclusion but, just maybe, he could arrange for a few more Arabs to end up dead in the final body count.

CHAPTER TWENTY-THREE➔

(I)

THE RENTED YACHT HARDLY BREACHED the mouth of the harbor before a gunboat joined it. Manned artillery aimed threateningly toward the sleek pleasure craft.

A man in military uniform hailed the yacht with a bullhorn. Chad couldn't understand the Arabic.

The yacht slowed. Within seconds, more gunboats joined the flotilla.

The yacht was escorted to Garuna. Immediately, an army of Arabs with 38/49 sub-machine guns took positions to prevent any unauthorized disembarkations.

(II)

FIRST, LENARD COHEN HAD COMMITTED SUICIDE, when Raziz had been convinced the Jew was a gutless wonder safe with one live shot.

Now, whether Wayne's story turned out to be true or not, it offered too much opportunity to resist.

How clever of the Jew to make *the bomb* an a-bomb. How could Raziz resist the temptation of that? Even though, as the Jew undoubtedly knew and planned, it would be Arab against Arab in the game fought for possession.

CHAPTER TWENTY-FOUR➜

(I)

THE ROOM WAS SILENT EXCEPT for staccato from the radio receiver.

Meyer Bregrael's eyes were on the radio operator.

"Gibberish!" the radio man said finally.

"Meyer felt the painful knotting of his guts. Something was wrong, and he and his guts knew it.

(II)

RAMILE MOHAMMED LISTENED. He was especially interested, because the "package" convoy, at that very moment, was leaving Garuna for Mahud Wadi.

"Can we trace it?" he asked.

"Only if it continues," Arras Sebdat answered.

Ramile was tempted to delegate someone else to follow through. Probably, he should be more concerned with what was happening on the road, but this radio "business" had, he readily admitted, become a personal obsession.

He left Ma'homet Alhid in charge of convoy security.

106

He took twenty-four men and veered toward deep desert.

His equipment for tracking the ongoing signal was the best that Arab Petrodollars could buy.

He became more nervous with each minute that the signal continued. What was so important that sender and receiver were now on the verge of betraying the former's exact location?

His truck headed south when a more direct line became impossible because of the terrain.

Through the windshield, nothing seemed alive, although Ramile knew his eyes lied. There were two-legged Jewish animals out there; harbingers of the danger he felt deep in his bowels.

His truck skirted the rim of a deep gully, finally able to head southwest again. The signal became more distinct.

His truck stopped. His experienced ears listened.

"Just over the next dune." Arras Sebdat predicted and motioned toward the high pile of gray sand directly in their pathway.

Ramile divided his men into three groups of eight. One group would circle, from each side, pincher-like, the third up and over the top.

Ramile went with the left-flanking group; it would be difficult to attack from the top without being spotted.

As anticipated, the group atop the dune was the first to check in.

"Positive." Arras's voice sounded hollow over the walkie-talkie. "One tent. Whip antenna. No vehicles evident. No activity. No visible lookouts. Shall we move in?"

"Hold."

To Ramile's chagrin, his flanking movement was difficult to achieve. It was the other group who checked in next. "Sabin Shir duplicated the information already received, and Ramile again gave instructions to hold.

Then, he ordered his group up the massive sand wedge they hadn't yet been able to circumnavigate.

What greeted him was exactly as twice reported.

He unhooked his walkie-talkie from his belt.

"Top group, continue to hold. Flanking formations to the target area. Advance at will."

Ramile's approach was over exposed ground, but he wanted to be in on the kill. Keeping as low a profile as the terrain made possible, he and his men moved in prescribed zigzag.

Ramile was sweating, his 38/49 sub-machine gun at the ready as he motioned his men into the tent with him.

He hit the inside ground and rolled to a firing position. Adrenaline pumped through his veins.

The scene that greeted him was as absurd as it was unexpected.

A giant of an Arab sat stark naked on a rug before a radio. His left hand played with the transmitter key. His right hand fondled his exposed and monstrously aroused genitalia.

"Gramal," the giant introduced himself, and his idiot face broke into an idiot grin.

In the distance, there was an audible rumble that Ramile had no difficulty whatsoever in identifying.

(III)

RAZIZ HADN'T EXPECTED the head of Mahud Wadi security personally to follow up on the ruse provided by Gramal and the Jewish radio, but there was still plenty of resistance left for him to deal with at the convoy.

He'd carefully picked his spot to attack, because it wasn't obviously ideal for an ambush. Not that the convoy would be expecting trouble. More likely, it would have seemed highly unlikely that any sizable Jewish assault group could have penetrated so far into Arab territory without detection. It would have been inconceivable to the average Arab that he might purposely be set upon by his brothers in Islam.

There were several helicopters in use by the Mahud Wadi contingent, each with the latest equipment. Raziz was gambling that none of those would risk firing off their supplemental sophisticated weaponry in such close proximity to the a-bomb.

CHAPTER TWENTY-FIVE➔

(I)

SURPRISED WAS AN UNDERSTATEMENT. One minute, Chad was seated in the truck, hearing Ali's comments on the scenery. The next minute, their driver's mouth bubbled bloody red froth, and the truck veered sharply toward the side of the embankment.

Chad and Ali in unison grabbed too late for the errant wheel. The truck lurched and tipped onto its passenger side.

Chad was buried beneath Ali and the dead driver. The latter still spasmed and leaked blood everywhere.

The truck windshield was a mass of spider-web cracks.

Ali's heavy breathing was punctuated by twig-snapping shots fired from single rifles. Suddenly, there were the accompanying short staccato burps of automatic weapons' fire.

There was an explosion.

Chad smelled gas and struggled. His hands, face, and clothes were wet with blood he could only hope wasn't even partly his own.

110

There was more gunfire. Someone shouted in Arabic that Chad didn't understand.

Chad stepped on the dead driver's face on the way by, and collapsing cheek bone crunched beneath the exerted force of his boot.

Air. He took a deep gulp of it. It came into his lungs saturated with diesel fumes.

His head poked through the open window, the rest of his body still wedged by the driver's dead-weight.

Ali, who had climbed free ahead of Chad, stumbled around in a daze.

Downed men sprawled everywhere in grotesque attitudes of death.

There was more machine-gun fire and a resulting row of splattered dust that moved in a line all of the way to the tipped truck. Chad thought he saw death racing to greet him until the very second it passed him by.

The metal of the door was hot; Chad burned his hands and forearms as he fought for leverage to pry him free of his potential coffin.

Once out, though, he, like Ali, hadn't the foggiest notion of what to do next.

Bullets danced the dirt at his feet and put him into a reflexive run. Ali was forgotten until Chad reached temporary protection beside a smoking Jeep.

The truck Chad had just deserted erupted in an eyebrow-singeing fireball.

Chad thought he saw Ali in a slight depression by the side of the road. He went to join him.

He landed with a hard plop that took his breath away.

His companion, just joined, wasn't Ali. While there were no visible signs of trauma, there was no mistaking a corpse when seen.

Chad relieved the victim of a PPS43 and Beretta M51 and left with them.

He passed empty trucks and Jeeps, looking for Ali.

Arabs (enemies? friends?) were crouched mainly outside their vehicles.

"A helicopter flew low over the convoy. As long as it wasn't firing at him, Chad found its presence psychologically comforting.

He had never used an 82 cm, 3.6 kg., 7.62 mm PP543 with its 35-round, banana-shaped magazine. He hoped all he needed to do was aim, line up the target along the front sight, and squeeze off the trigger. When he did just that, the resulting barrage cut the man in half who had looked way too unfriendly in his screaming run towards Chad.

Chad adjusted his erection into a more comfortable position after he dropped between the rear wheels of the a-bomb transport.

The bomb sat, covered with tarp, on the flatbed directly above him. Possibly, no one fired in Chad's direction, because no one knew for sure what would happen if a stray bullet hit the ancient a-bomb.

Chad had fleeting thoughts of exploding the bomb, right then and there. Mahud Wadi was close enough so bomb radioactivity, shock wave, blast, and/or fireball would do irreparable damage. But Chad wasn't enthused about dying quite yet. He had a boner that needed milking, first.

Someone had risked enough shots to kill the Arab dangling half in and half out of the truck cab.

Chad grabbed the corpse's dangling right arm and gave a tug. The body, going stiff, completed its fall.

Chad looked inside. The truck keys were still in the ignition.

He started the truck, put it in gear, and drove it out of the convoy.

The door on the passenger side jerked open. An Arab tried his best to join Chad inside. Friend Arab? Enemy Arab? Chad didn't know. Chad didn't care. He was prepared to blow the dark-skinned son-of-a-bitch to Kingdom Come.

"Don't you dare shoot me, you bastard!" It was Ali who completed his climb inside and slammed the door shut behind him.

(II)

THERE WERE REASONS THE SOLDIERS guarding the convoy didn't provide a more coordinated front.

Ramile Mohammed, around whom everyone would have logically rallied, wasn't there.

His second-in-command, Ma'homet Alhid, was one of the three men riding in the lead Jeep and taken out at the get-go.

Riad Bahid, the remaining member of the security triumvirate, had remained at Garuna.

(III)

THE HELICOPTER moved after Raziz's Jeep and the truck.

The chopper gunner took too long to capitalize on his advantage.

Raziz squeezed off an AK47 assault rifle and emptied the total contents of its magazine into the pursuing aircraft. His companion in the backseat did the same.

The helicopter pulled upward briefly, paused dramatically, tilted precariously, and fell catastrophically out of the sky.

(IV)

CHAD SAW THE EXPLOSION, felt its heat, fought the truck as the shock wave vibrated the ground.

There was so much dust that Chad and Ali were almost too late in realizing Raziz's Jeep was almost passed them.

Chad jerked the wheel to the left to move the transport truck directly into the middle of the roadway.

A deep ravine opened on the driver's side of the road, and Chad turned the truck to drive the lane opposite.

The ravine made a quick right-angle and shot off in its new direction.

Ali fired at the Jeep and the three men inside it. Again, his target disappeared into the dust. When it reappeared, its passengers numbered only two. Simultaneously, unfamiliar sounds were heard on the roof of the truck cab.

Ali aimed the barrel of his revolver straight up and fired twice.

A hand appeared, curled around the top of the window on Ali's side.

Ali beat the fingers with the butt of his pistol and turned them to bloody mush before they slid away. Blood suddenly dripped the windshield.

Ali roof-fired again. An arm cascaded from the roof and an attached hand methodically clutched at the bloody glass immediately in front of Chad's face. A shoulder slid into appearance, then half a face; the other half of which had been shot away.

Chad suddenly couldn't see a damned thing *but* dangling body parts and accompanying smears of greasy blood.

He reached his left arm out of the driver's window and rose up out of his seat for the stretch needed for his fingers to find and grab wet corpse hair. He yanked.

The body slid the windshield to straddle the hood.

In the interim, Raziz's Jeep passed and now began a seemingly uncontrolled spin in the center of the road immediately in front of them.

When hit by the truck, the Jeep slid sideways and tipped, spilling its remaining two occupants. The forward momentum of the truck pushed the smaller vehicle toward the left and into a stone embankment.

There was a pyrotechnical display of sparks and a cacophony of grating *crunch*.

The Jeep irretrievably lodged between stone and truck to force both vehicles into a jarring stop.

Ali was thrown forward. His forehead hit the windshield—hard.

(V)

IT TOOK CHAD PRECIOUS SECONDS to realize he was alive and that the inside of his crotch was wet with excitement-orgasmed semen.

Ali was still breathing but unconscious and wedged between the truck seat and the dashboard.

Beretta M51 in hand, Chad opened the door and came out in a low crouch.

The silence, so intense after the grinding of metal against metal and against stone, dissolved in the distant thunder from a battle still in progress in the distance.

Chad moved cautiously and quickly.

The unnatural twist of Raziz's left leg said it was broken. However, a broken leg didn't necessarily immobilize an enemy.

Raziz groaned.

Chad was tempted to put him out of his misery. In fact, he would have derived great satisfaction, sexual and otherwise, in doing just that. Except he'd just ejaculated and needed at least a few moments for his cock to re-swell and, besides, there was a possible advantage in having at least one hostage; the other Arab, who'd been still along for the ride, was definitely dead.

Chad searched Raziz and found two knives and a French-made M50 pistol. He used Raziz's own belt to hog-tie him.

He turned his attention back to the truck.

The bomb had shifted enough on impact to snap one restraining cable. A section of its once-concealing tarp was undone and twisted to reveal metal.

Chad ran to the truck trailer and lifted himself up onto the flatbed and, only then, discovered the a-bomb he'd accompanied from Mahud Wadi was a fake.

(VI)

IN THE DISTANCE, GUNS STILL FIRED, but not nearly as much as before.

Ali was still unconscious, dead-weight as Chad maneuvered him into position to tie his wrists. Chad gagged him and wrapped Ali's head in the man's own shirt.

Chad returned to Raziz and delivered two sharp slaps to the face.

"Come on, bastard! Come on!"

Raziz seemed reluctant to regain consciousness.

"Goddamn it, I said wake up!"

Raziz's eyes fluttered and opened.

"Do you speak English?" Chad wasn't encouraged by Raziz's vacant stare. "English, you son-of-a-bitch. Do you speak English?"

Whether he could or not, Raziz shook his head.

"Christ!" Chad grabbed handfuls of Raziz's shirt and yanked him to a sitting position.

The Arab grunted. His forehead beaded sweat.

"I'm your friend," Chad shouted into Raziz's bewildered and flushed face. "I'm going to help you, but you have to help me get you to the truck and get you in it. Do you understand? I can't move you far on your own, because you're too fucking heavy as dead-weight."

Chad hooked his arms beneath Raziz's arms. He miraculously managed to bring a suddenly cooperating Raziz to a standing position.

The Arab appeared on the brink of another mental and physical black-out, most likely pure survival instinct what moved him, dragging his broken leg, when Chad moved.

Raziz vomited from the strain and pain. The resulting mess splattered them both and saturated the air with a heavy sweet-sour smell.

"Jesus!" Chad puked in sympathetic reflex.

Raziz threatened to slide one trail of smelly stomach contents, all of the way to the ground, but rallied at the last minute.

"You have to get up into the cab of the truck." Chad said; easier said than done.

Raziz expended the last of his energy to comply, succeeded with Chad's help, and then pass out.

Chad slid behind the wheel, almost overcome by the stench of sweat, blood, and vomit. Suddenly, too, there were flies summoned from God-only-knew-where.

He shifted the truck gears into neutral and engaged the starter. The engine turned but didn't take.

"Come on, you hunk of metallic shit!"

The motor caught, sputtered, stalled, caught, sputtered, stalled, and…caught.

Chad put the truck in reverse and backed up.

He geared into first and turned the wheels sharply to ease the truck not toward Mahud Wadi but into deeper desert.

He only hoped Raziz would regain consciousness soon enough, long enough, to give Chad some badly needed directions, or Chad's half-assed plan wouldn't have the chance of a snowball in hell.

CHAPTER TWENTY-SIX➔

(I)

ALAN WAYNE HEARD THE COMMOTION. In the dark, tied, he was unable to define it.

For the first time, he felt some of the frustration that saw Lenard Cohen put a gun into his mouth and pull the trigger. Still, if Alan had gun, he would have been more inclined to kill an Arab than himself.

He tried again to get free.

There weren't that many Arabs in camp, most having moved out to intercept the bomb convoy en route to Mahud Wadi.

On the other hand, where would he go? The only inhabitants of the immediate area were likely hostile Arabs more likely to cut his throat than provide succor.

He should just thank God that he was alive.

He shut his eyes, disturbed to be so tired. Sleeping away the last of his hours would be unproductive waste.

Tent flaps parted.

"Up, Jew!"

Alan opened his eyes and got up.

120

The Arab untied the rope end attached to the stone weight, but not the end that tied Alan's wrists behind him.

The Arab held to the free end and nodded Alan outside, like a man about to walk his dog.

Alan wondered if his time had come and who, back home, would ever know he'd met his fate behind some desert sand dune, the slug of a Beretta M51 lodged in his brain.

Another Arab was outside with a Carl Gustav M45B sub-machine gun, Swedish design, licensed for manufacturer in Egypt. The permanent magazine housing contained 36 rounds of 9mm Parabellum.

"Come on, move ass, Jew!" insisted Arab number one.

Alan saw the stretch of camouflage netting over the diesel truck parked on the edge of the camp.

It seemed impossible that Raziz had somehow wrestled from superior forces the bomb on that truck's flatbed.

"Eyes forward!"

Alan got the barrel of the machine gun poked between his shoulder blades for emphasis.

The camp was four tents and a cave in wind-carved in sandstone. The Arabs, together and in unison, pushed Alan into one tent; they stayed outside.

Raziz reclined on a floor rug. There were several cushions tucked beneath his left armpit. To one side was an Arab with 38/49 aimed in Alan's direction.

There was someone (blond?), almost completely hidden within the shadows.

"Ah, Jew." Raziz said in Arabic, and his voice broke with the pain of his wound festering beneath the blanket he'd drawn up to conceal it. "You will ask this young American who he is and what he wants from me."

Alan caught a good look of Chad for the first time and recognized him.

"Do you speak English?" Chad didn't recognize Alan, yet another fellow University of Washington classmate, through the swelling of the Jew's many cuts and bruises. His ignorance was helped by hardly expecting Alan anywhere near.

"The Arab guy, here, wants to know who you are and what you want from him," Alan said.

"Ask him *who he is* and what he wants *from me*," Chad countered.

"His name is Bara Raziz. He's Palestinian."

"What are you two saying, Jew?" Raziz insisted.

"He wants to know who you are," Alan translated. "I told him."

"I'm the one asking the questions." Raziz's face scrunched in determination and pain.

"You might want to oblige him with an answer," Alan said to Chad in English. "He can get very nasty if he cares to be."

Raziz's impatience didn't improve.

"Well?" he demanded.

"Tell him I'm sympathetic to his cause," Chad said. "When the opportunity presented itself, I took advantage. Things are often less complicated than they seem."

Raziz listened to Alan's translation of what Chad had said but found it hard to believe the young American had so quickly—and so inexplicably—pulled Raziz's ass from defeat to victory.

122

"What was he doing in the convoy?" Raziz used the back of his hand to wipe away the sweat accumulated on his forehead.

"I'm responsible for the bomb having been delivered at Garuna in the first place," Chad said.

"*You?*" No way had Alan controlled *his* anger and amazement.

Chad still didn't realize Alan and he had known each other before.

"What exactly are *you* doing in the camp of Arab Bara Raziz, Jew?" Chad was suddenly curious.

Alan remembered and regretted the lust he'd once felt for this traitor, no matter how handsome, to Israel.

"You bastard!" he finally spat and, despite his hands still tied, made a move to take Chad down.

The barrel of the Arab guard's 38/49 came down hard along the side of Alan's head. He dropped to his knees. His spine telescoped. He was kicked face down and held there by the Arab boot placed between his shoulder blades.

He twisted his head to Chad.

"*You* killed Martha, didn't you, you son-of-a-bitch, and put the blame on me!" Alan accused.

"Jesus H. Christ! Alan Wayne?"

Alan tried to get to his feet but the gun barrel, jabbed painfully into the base of his skull, kept him put.

"You're going to ruin everything for your side if you keep this up," Chad warned.

"You're fucking crazy!" Having once allowed his defenses to slip with this duplicitous bastard, Alan had no intentions of letting it ever happen a second time.

Raziz was furious in being left out of the conversation and looked it.

"Shut the fuck up, both of you!"

"Better play along with me, Alan," Chad said; he flashed Raziz a winning smile.

"Listen to me, Jew." Raziz's attention was fully on Alan. "You will say nothing except what I tell you to say. If you do otherwise, I'll see that you're put out of your misery, here and now."

Alan glared across the distance at Chad.

"The young American shit says he's responsible for the bomb having been delivered at Garuna."

Alan realized Chad had probably been in the a-bomb business from the get-go.

"Ask him why he has turned the bomb over *to me?*" Raziz instructed.

"I felt the original buyers were unprepared to put the bomb to its best use," Chad said.

Raziz recognized flattery when he heard it. However if what Chad said wasn't true, what was? There was no denying the American had delivered the bomb to Raziz.

"Tell Mr. Raziz that he should immediately inform the who-haws at Mahud Wadi that he has captured not only Chad Nordell but Ali Bahid, the brother of Riad Bahid.

When so told, Raziz's surprise was jaw-dropping

"He should inform Mahud Wadi that he has persuaded me to activate the bomb," Chad continued, "so they should try to wrest the bomb from him only if they're prepared for the consequences."

"What in the fuck are you up to?" Alan asked; Raziz frowned and grunted a warning. Alan passed on what Chad said.

Raziz looked at Chad with awe and continued suspicion.

"I've counted only four men in camp, Alan," Chad said casually. "How many are there, *exactly*."

"Five." Alan didn't have a clue what Chad was up to.

"What did the American say?" Raziz wanted to know.

"He's hungry and tired. He hopes you'll provide him with something to eat and a bed in which to rest his weary bones."

Raziz found it frustrating and inconvenient to have this slippery Jew as an intermediary.

The American, though, *did* look tired, as might be expected.

(II)

IT WAS NO MORE DIFFICULT for Chad to kill the Arab assigned guard duty outside Ali's tent than it had been for him to kill the Arab assigned guard duty outside Alan's tent, although separately nor combined had these last two killings provided him a spontaneous orgasm. He wondered if he was already getting jaded, encouraged only by how painfully swollen the death throes of those Arabs had made his dick.

No one had expected him so quickly and unexpectedly to begin taking back what he had so magnanimously just delivered.

He relieved dead-man two of his 38/49, even if he knew using the gun would cut down his odds of success.

He would, also, be in deep shit if Alan's head count of Raziz's men was off by even one.

He took several very deep breaths and told himself to be calm.

Things could have turned out far more difficult. Not that he was home free. It was dangerous and premature to imagine himself already in the truck, already speeding across the desert. There were obstacles that still needed eliminating each and every step of the way.

(III)

ALI HAD A SPLITTING HEADACHE, made no less so by his attempts to put mental order to the events which brought him into the enemy camp.

Correctly, he suspected he had struck his head against the windshield or dashboard of the Chad-crashed truck. After that, he'd been blindfolded and gagged and had listened to some Arab grunting directions to Chad who apparently was driving.

Finally taken out of the truck, he had been manhandled and unceremoniously deposited inside a tent (he thought) and left to wonder why. He heard occasional bits of muted conversations that left him none the wiser with their reference to "the bomb", someone called "Raziz", and "the blond American" (Chad?).

He remained concerned about Chad. The poor bastard had probably been scared shitless when he'd rammed the truck carrying the a-bomb into the Jeep.

126

If Chad had made it this far, it was doubtful he'd forgive Ali for getting him involved. What Chad had joined into, likely thinking it would just be a college-boys' lark, had metamorphosed into something dangerously life-threatening.

Ali needed more information. It was easier to deal with any problem if all of the facts were known. He couldn't even be sure who his enemy was, although Arabic was the only language being spoken within earshot.

There was the sound of someone entering. More movement of someone kneeling. Deft fingers began unfastening the ties that held the makeshift hood around Ali's head.

"Surprise!"

"Chad?" Ali's surprise was muted by his gag.

"Shhhh!" Chad put his index finger against his lips.

He removed Ali's gag.

"What in the hell is happening?" Ali's words were slurred by his mouth made numb by lengthy stuffing.

"We're the good guys escaping the bad. The camp has only a skeleton crew, the rest not scheduled to straggle on in from the convoy ambush until morning."

"How in the fuck do you know that? How in the fuck did you get free?"

"My, you are just full of questions." Chad had no intention of fabricating explanations at this point.

Ali massaged circulation back into his wrists while Chad untied his ankles.

THE GOMORRHA CONJURATIONS, BY WILLIAM MALTESE

"I hope you're going to be able to walk, buddy," Chad said, "or we're going to be in deep shit without a shovel."

"I'll walk. You can damn well count on it."

"There's no way we're getting the bomb back to Mahud Wadi by any kind of direct route," Chad said.

Ali stopped rubbing.

"The minute we pull out of here with the bomb," Chad said, "there isn't going to be a bad guy within miles who isn't going to know where we're headed."

"You're not suggesting we leave it here?" Ali could see Chad thinking to save his neck, at the expense of forfeiting the bomb, but he surely didn't think Ali would be won over to any such plan of action.

"What if one of us hides the bomb while the other goes to Mahud Wadi for help?" Chad suggested. "The bad guys will be so busy looking for two men in a truck with a bomb, one of us can surely slip passed them.

"Where in the hell could either of us hide something as big as the bomb?"

"I'm thinking I could drive it into deeper desert. Who would expect that? Meanwhile, you get to the fortress for help and head on back to pick up your lover and the bomb your lover is herding."

"And how in the hell would I ever find you?"

"Oh, you'd find me. However, that said, you have to promise me one thing, on your father's grave."

"What?"

"That you *will* be back for me, even if you have to come alone."

"That I promise you. I swear. On my father's grave, may he rest in peace."

(IV)

RAZIZ CALLED FOR YUSSEF. He didn't know what he needed, but he had to have something to get his mind off the pain, even if was just the distraction of someone, anyone, *being there*. He tried to throw back his blanket, only to fail. The material, stiff with blood, stuck to his wound. His sense of smell picked up the tell-tale aroma of his flesh gone or going sour.

Another surge of agony shot his leg and caused additional sweat on his forehead. Liquid ran into his eyes and along his nose.

"Yussef, you bastard, get in here!"

It wasn't Yussef, though, who answered his call.

"You!" No denying Raziz's surprise. "How…?"

Alan relieved Raziz's pain and suffering, once and for all.

CHAPTER TWENTY-SEVEN →

(I)

IT WAS FRATRICIDE.

Oh, Riad Bahid hadn't actually pulled the trigger to kill his brother, but he *had* sent Ali to his death as surely as the sun would come up in the morning.

Riad took cheer in how rationalization could always be found even for such a horrendous crime as this one. In that, of course, Riad had to send Ali, and Ali's handsome American lover off, as part of the doomed convoy. To have done otherwise might have raised the suspicions of the enemy.

Defining "the enemy" was difficult. The Jews were the enemy. The Palestinians were a potential enemy; reports having indicated they were possibility within the restricted zone.

Riad tired to picture how it had been when his brother and the American had so bravely commandeered the fake bomb and drove off with it into the sunset. What an unnecessary display of theatrics! How, though, could Ali or the American have known, since Riad, for security reasons, hadn't made either of them privy to his plans.

130

If Ali and the American had just stayed low, the rebels would have been defeated; they turned out to be a very small band, indeed. Or, they would have ended up stealing a bogus bomb.

Maybe it all would have played out differently if Ali and Riad had been more brothers than just acquaintances. Had Riad known Ali better, he might have better anticipated his brother's heroic reaction to the attack on the convoy. However, the two siblings had never been close; first Riad had gone off to attend foreign schools, then Ali had headed off for his training and education. The two brothers were seldom in the same place at the same time. Ali's arrival at Garuna was their first reunion in five years.

Would Ali have allowed Riad to go off on the convoy if their roles had been reversed?

As for the American, about whom Riad knew next to nothing, except that he was sleeping in Ali's bed, and had assisted Ali in getting the real bomb to Mahud Wadi, there'd been no possible way for Riad to have foreseen the how and why of *his* jumping into the truck cab and starting off, Ali hopping aboard.

Was Riad jealous of those two? He was no stranger to male-male attraction. His defining moment had occurred in France. It had quickly ended when Riad's father had made it perfectly clear that certain same-sex affairs simply couldn't tolerated. The very idea of Yasir Bahid's older son in love with a gay infidel was *completely* outside the boundaries of acceptability.

Riad's relationship with his father had deteriorated steadily after Paris. Riad had remained bitter, masochistically eliminating all affection—for his father, for Ali, for any man, for any woman—from his life.

What would his father think if he were resurrected to discover Ali, too, had succumbed to the temptation of homosexuality? Would Yasir Bahid have looked upon Ali's affair differently because Ali wasn't the older son?

(II)

HUSSEIN NAZREDDIN SURVEYED THE DESERTED campsite in the dawn of the new day.

Pale sun filtered out the glare that would prevail later, sand and sandstone now bathed in a kind of milky opaqueness relieved only by the four dun-colored tents. A pile of camouflage netting was discarded nearby, concealing nothing but the ground beneath it.

A breeze stirred and sent billows of dust whipping around.

Hussein suspected Bara Raziz had recognized the risk of holding the bomb in a locale so vulnerably exposed to discovery as this one.

Hussein thanked whatever fates allowed him to view the quickly disappearing truck tracks before they were completely swept away. With luck, future generations would point to his name and remember how he had gone into the deep desert with Bara Raziz to guard with his life that prize which was destined to return Arabs victorious to Palestine.

He mounted his camel and urged the sitting beast to its feet.

He rode southward, unknowingly passing over the shallow grave of Bara Raziz as he did so.

CHAPTER TWENTY-EIGHT➔

(I)

ALI SPOTTED THE SMALL GROUP of Palestinians. He remained hidden from them within a maze of dirt pillars formed by some long-ago rush of rare flood water from nearby high ground.

Although he was eventually able to sneak away in the darkness, he lost valuable time and still had miles to go.

He was beginning to question his chances for survival, let alone success. It had been years since he'd challenged the uncompromising desert terrain and won.

(II)

NOT TOUCHING, ALAN WAYNE, now out of hiding, and Chad were on the truck flatbed, heads laid against one of the large wooden blocks that braced the cylindrical cargo.

Stars were startling pinpoints in the blanket-black of the sky. If a moon was scheduled, it hadn't arrived and showed no signs of doing so any time soon.

"You're sure Riad Bahid didn't trust you?" Alan's voice sounded unnaturally loud in the parenthesizing desert silence.

"He didn't even trust his own brother, as it turned out, did he, sending him off with me and a fake bomb? I figure my chances of accessing the real bomb at the fortress were suddenly next to nothing. Even if I got into the fortress, what kind of valid excuse was I going to give to see the bomb again?

Alan still smarted in Chad having never been who or what he'd seemed to be.

Chad had known all about the Arab purchase the a-bomb from Harold, Martha, and Randolph. Hell, he'd cleverly set up Alan for Martha's murder.

"I did my job. I'm a secret agent, *licensed to kill*," Chad had validated."

"Did you ever really care for me?" Alan was a glutton for punishment."

Chad turned in his direction and shifted position to get warmer. It was always so cold at night in desert so hot during the day. The only periods that managed to be comfortable were the couple of minutes just after sunset and sunrise.

"You're fishing for compliments, are you?" Alan smiled.

"More a case of professional pride. I hate thinking I was so completely taken in."

"Of course I had feelings for you. Still do. Why else set you free and bring you with me?"

Alan, though, couldn't help but wonder if he heard the obviously malleable Chad once again merely adjusting to changed circumstances.

"An awfully lot hinges on Ali coming back for you, doesn't it?" Alan changed the subject.

"There's certainly no guarantee, but he does believe I saved his life, proved myself more than once by putting my life on the line for his cause, and he did give me his solemn word, on his father's grave, that he'll be back for me."

"We live in times when a man's word doesn't necessarily mean shit."

"We can wave good-bye to our sorry asses, then."

(III)

SCREAMS.

Ramile Mohammed had ordered the interrogations, because he felt personally responsible for Ali missing.

Riad Bahid had assured Ramile that, all things considered, Ramile had *not* been lax in leaving the convoy to seek out and identify the source of the radio signals. However, Ramile felt certain that had he stayed with the convoy, he would have prevented Riad's brother from joining in with the American's useless heroics.

He could only hope Ali was still alive.

He considered it favorable that the sudden cessation of screams was so soon followed by the appearance of Sabin Sahir.

Sabin Sahir was genuinely pleased, and had every right to be. He had obtained the information Ramile wanted.

(IV)

THE COLD WAS MERELY an excuse. Even without it, they would have found one another. After all, they had less and less chance of surviving beyond the next couple of days, and there were few enough pleasures to be had between then and now.

Granted, Alan toyed with the idea of not letting it happen, deriving a masochistic pleasure in thinking he could master abstinence. He still smarted from how Chad had used him.

In the end, though, it was ridiculous to hold grudges which, in affect, would cut off his nose to spite his face. Chad's betrayal, what-seemed-a-hundred-years-ago, though a blow to Alan's ego, was nothing Alan probably wouldn't have done in Chad's shoes.

A greater obstacle was Alan's fear that sex, now, might destroy the illusion of how good he still imagined sex would have been for them, before.

Still, no matter what happened in the past, the two were definitely on the same side, here and now. There was no denying the sexual attraction between them, only intensified by their dire circumstances.

In the end, lost in the taste, the smell, and the feel of Chad's hungry masculinity, Alan could only shudder at how he had even temporarily considered depriving himself of such exquisite ecstasy before dying.

CHAPTER TWENTY-NINE➔

(I)

EVEN AS ALI BAHID VOMITTED, he knew he couldn't afford the loss of moisture.

He had gambled and lost. Unable to keep down the brackish, slime-covered water, he regurgitated even more of it to splash dust-covered stones with green bile.

Where was the peace, the tranquility, the relieving euphoria promised at the moment of death? All he felt was anger that it should end this way for him.

He was too young to die. At eighty, he might have been tired of life, not now.

He had faced death before, but he had never, until now, *really* believed he would become victim to it.

Would Chad believe that Ali had died still trying to reach Mahud Wadi?

His belly cramping with even more pain, Ali convulsed into wracking dry heaves.

(II)

THERE WAS STILL FUEL left in the tank, but it wasn't enough for the truck to get far. Therefore,

Alan and Chad parked themselves, the truck, the remaining fuel, and the fake a-bomb, on a ridge, where all could be spotted by their still-hoped-for rescuers.

They used the bomb tarp as an awning from the sun, but the resulting shadows within were heat-filled and left them sweaty even before they stripped to their under shorts.

They fought any urge for more water, their supply running out.

"There's someone out there," Alan said. "I can feel him there."

Several times, since yesterday, he'd made the same Pollyannaish statement. As before, Chad surveyed the horizon and saw not a damned thing but sand.

Even if there was, that someone would have revealed himself by now—if friendly.

A river of sweat cascaded the narrow valley between Chad's pectorals and pooled within the scalloped ridges of his muscled belly. His navel overflowed with his salty body fluid.

Despite the heat, he shivered.

(III)

HUSSEIN NAZREDDIN SLID THE SLOPE of gray sand and crawled into his small lean-to made of two sticks draped by his caftan.

He was confused. Having finally managed a rendezvous with the truck and a-bomb, he found not his leader, Bara Raziz, but the Jew who Raziz had captured in the trap baited by the other Jew, Lenard Cohen.

This Jew wasn't alone, either, although Hussein had no idea who his companion was. If he had a vague recollection of a blond head amidst the enemy forces, during the attack on the convoy, he didn't make that connection, now. He hadn't been well-positioned to observe Chad and Ali having maneuvered the truck and bomb from the convoy.

There could be no question about this truck, being *the* truck. The tarp, now pulled back slightly, revealed part of the deadly cylinder behind the seated young men.

So, where was Bara Raziz? Where were the others? Why had this Jew and this handsome blond brought the bomb here of all places? They were making no attempt to hide it. Quite to the contrary, truck and trailer were hard to miss.

Hussein had no easy time putting two and two together and never did manage to come up with four. He only knew that if the Jew was in charge (and there was no indication that he was restrained), something was wrong. Hussein's dilemma was only what to do about it.

Killing the Jew and the blond were certainly very good options. However, where did Hussein go from there? Having found empty diesel cans discarded along the truck route, the vehicle couldn't have the fuel to go much farther. Was the Jew counting on fuel pumps springing up out of the wilderness?

Hussein settled back into his cramped confines, long experience allowing him successfully to ignore the heat, the stickiness, the stink of his body, and the buzz of the horsefly apparently conjured from nothing for no other purpose than to annoy one of the three men who had passed this way in a decade.

He shut his eyes, determined to get whatever rest he could. He would go closer to the truck and its occupants after nightfall. He refused the demands of his stomach to drink or eat. He was, after all, a long way from the nearest natural source of potable water and supplies. He doubted the Jew and the blond would willingly share whatever food or water had traveled into the wilderness with them.

(IV)

CHAD KNEW WHAT ALAN WAS DOING. He objected.

"I'm not going to let that bastard sneak up and pick us off at his pleasure," Alan said.

"You go wandering around after dark, and I won't know where to find you until the buzzards start circling" Unlike Alan, Chad wasn't convinced there was anyone or anything (two-legged, four-legged, no-legged) within miles.

"Grown attached to me, have you?"

"I just don't want to lose my toy-boy to paranoia."

"Nothing is going to happen to me if I have anything to say about it."

"What makes you think you'll have any say in the matter?"

"You started out solo; you might as well end up that way."

"I'd feel better with your continued company, thank you very much."

"I'm flattered."

"You're just too good sex to lose."

"Would you rather we were both killed in our sleep, or while fucking?"

"There are worst ways to go, but I do admit to preferring we not be killed at all."

"The least I can do is see you have every chance of getting back to Mahud Wadi if your friend pulls a no-show," Alan said. "Up until now, I've been along for the ride."

"So, what say I join you on this proposed snipe hunt of yours?"

"You'll stay right here. It may just be, you know, that the only reason we've been lucky so far is that whomever is out there thinks any stray bullet is going to set off fireworks." Alan patted the smooth metal cylinder.

"If that's the case, why play hero?"

"Maybe I don't want to see you get all the glory."

"Right."

"Just think of the satisfaction I'm going to get from doing my part."

He took one of the 38/49s and disappeared into the deeper darkness beneath the tarp. A few seconds later, he dropped to the sand on the other side of the transport.

Chad picked up a gun and cradled it.

(V)

THE MOON WASN'T DUE for another hour, although there was already an evident paleness on the horizon where it would eventually rise.

Chad was nervous, despite himself, finally infected by Alan's suspicions that they were being watched.

He leaned against the metal and tried to detect any movement within the darkness all around him.

The desert could be spooky at night: a black-and-white picture seen through diffusing cheese cloth.

Nothing heard, not even the wind. Very disturbing, since at least Alan *was* out there.

Chad rested chin upon the gun laid across his knees. His index finger nervously traced first one and then other of the weapon's dual trigger mechanism. This weapon was a far cry from the Colt .45 he'd used to blow away Harold Low. And where, he wondered, were Carol Hilliard and Joan Dunning? Did they even know what part they'd inadvertently played in all of this?

He was freezing. He was cramped. He was tired.

Was Alan merely hearing things as a result of the beatings he'd received from Raziz?

There was a sudden short burst of automatic gunfire.

Reflexively, Chad assumed a firing position.

He was surrounded by quiet made loud by it having been, albeit so briefly, interrupted.

An icy cold seeped his pores.

CHAPTER THIRTY→

(I)

"YOU'RE A FOOL!" RIAD BAHID stated, upon seeing his brother out of bed and dressing.

"I made a promise, on our father's grave," Ali said.

"You'll need days to get back on your feet."

"I'm back on my feet, now, or haven't you noticed? Besides, Chad doesn't have days."

"At least let somebody else go."

"I'm the only one, it seems, I can trust, aren't I?"

"It was Ramile Mohammed, after all, out looking on *my* instructions, who found you."

"And is Ramile Mohammed now out looking *for Chad* on your instructions?"

Riad frowned. Someone would pay dearly for Ali being so well informed.

"I could stop you, you know," Riad said. "Nothing enters or exits here without my say-so."

"But you won't stop me, will you?" Ali sat on the edge of the bed. The effort to pull on his boots was monumental. "You know why? You owe me for my having risked my neck to save for you what you'd falsely led me to believe was so damned important to you."

Chad, not Riad, had helped Ali survive the attack on the convoy *and* Ali's capture by Bara Raziz.

While Riad might successfully argue that he had acted without malice in sending Ali off in that convoy, he couldn't be one-hundred percent sure he hadn't been, and still wasn't, willing to sacrifice his brother's lover merely out of jealousy.

"Go on, then." He gave a could-care-less shrug.

"I have every intentions of doing so." Ali's last boot on, he was sweating profusely. He was sick to his stomach.

"You're not going to forgive me any time soon, are you?" Riad divined.

"I'm your brother. That should have counted for something." It was an accusation.

"It was a question of security. How was I to know you were going to take such risks?"

"I got the bomb to Garuna. Did you think I would willingly let it slip out of my fingers in convoy?"

"I merely took necessary precautions."

"You think you're some kind of clever hero, Riad? To me, you're still the same son-of-a-bitch who was too weak to tell our old man to mind his own business and get out of your sex life."

Riad's mouth dropped. Ali smirked.

"You didn't think that little scandal, involving you and your French kid was any big secret, did you? I could tell just what you were thinking when I got off that yacht and introduced you to Chad. Well, you fucking bastard, there's no way you're going to persuade me to throw Chad to the dogs like our old man persuaded you to toss away your frog. I've more guts in the what-I-want department and far-far bigger gonads."

"You really think I'd let the American die merely because of what's between you and him? Don't be absurd! I'm merely thinking how convenient if he and the bomb transport disappeared without a trace, leaving the Jews and the Palestinians both wondering if the bomb is lost forever."

"Bullshit! You're a closet faggot who finds it safer to masturbate than risk real relationships—with men, with women, with animals, even with me."

"You're not well, brother of mine. Too much sun makes you *decidedly* irrational."

"*Guilt,* brother, is what makes a man irrational. I can see guilt written across your face as if it were printed there in big red letters. You know very well that you hoped that neither Chad nor I would come back from that convoy. Me gone would free you completely, wouldn't it? You could wallow, forever and ever, Amen, in whatever masochistic joy you so obviously experience in being an emotional cripple. Now that you realize you didn't succeed in me dead, you think you'll somehow convince me to join you within whatever perverted lonely little corner you've walked yourself into."

"We live in a world where emotions are our enemies, little brother. You think I'm resentful that our father made me see the light by cutting off my relationship with Adrian? Hell no! He did me a favor, just like I'll do one for you, now, by letting this American of yours exit, here and now. Emotions make us vulnerable in times when the least weakness can destroy us all."

"Since when has Chad become the enemy? If it hadn't been for him, I wouldn't have gotten the bomb to Garuna."

"A chess game is often won by sacrificing pawns."

"I'm not your pawn in any damned chess game *you* may be playing. Neither is Chad."

"We're *all* pawns, brother, and the sooner you *and* your American paramour realize that, the better off we're all going to be."

(II)

OVERKILL: USING A GRENADE to kill an ant

All evidence pointed to Bara Raziz's little group having disbanded. Certainly, the few left didn't warrant the firepower of four TOW missiles on each side of the UH-1-B (Huey Cobra) helicopter. The M621 HMG heavy machine gun would have been more than enough.

Ali, though, was determined to arrive with all the pomp and circumstance of a rescuing hero.

(III)

"YOU'RE BLEEDING, AGAIN!"

"Am I?" Alan pretended his pain was less than it was. "Funny, I don't feel a thing."

"You're a liar and a goddamned fool to boot," Chad diagnosed.

"At least, we don't have to worry about getting our throats slit in the middle of the night.

"You'll probably end up dead anyway if we can't get the bleeding stopped. Besides, what makes you think the bastard you killed doesn't have friends waiting in the wings?"

"I'm counting on *your* friend arriving first."

Chad hated to admit it, but the possibilities were suddenly very good that Ali wasn't going to show.

"Haven't given up all hope of ever seeing him again, have you?" Alan literally felt the seepage of his blood into the makeshift bandage wrapping his ribcage. "It'd be a goddamned shame if we got this far and didn't make it to the finish.

"Great help you'll be even if Ali does show." Chad ripped another strip of cloth from his shirt and added it to the material covering Alan's wound.

Chad's bare torso was toasted deep mahogany and was glossed with glistening sweat.

"Don't worry any about me," Alan said. "I'm in great shape."

"And the Pope is Jewish."

"Is he?"

"Certainly I'm in better shape than that bastard who'd been out there waiting to sneak on up and slit our throats."

Chad just hoped Alan could hold out for just a little while longer. There was something to be said for the more dignified end of going out with a big bang as opposed to slowly bleeding to death in the middle of nowhere.

Chad scooted deeper into the hot shade and languidly stroked his ill-concealed erection.

(IV)

ALI SAW THE BUZZARDS before he saw the truck. The large birds, held aloft in heated desert air currents, circled in a narrowing and deepening downward spiral.

He wasn't prepared to be too late.

He took one last look at the surrounding terrain, assuring himself there was no visible enemy. He then left the helicopter and its pilot the moment the aircraft touched ground.

He slid sand and made noise to scatter the birds, many too glutted to fly.

He stopped when overcome by the intense smell of heat-baked decomposing human flesh.

The corpse was black and wore clothes holed by greedily pecking bird beaks. Eye sockets were drained—whether by the glaring sun or by the sipping buzzards wasn't clear. Black hair assured it wasn't Chad, although not even the victim's mother would recognize him now.

Back at the helicopter, Ali's pilot was suddenly out and waving his arms.

Ali drew his pistol. He expected the worst, somewhat encouraged by the pilot making no attempts to reenter the helicopter for a quick take-off.

Someone, Ali finally saw, was collapsed on the sand between the bomb transport truck and the helicopter.

Ali moved, frustrated by soft sand that made his progress so fucking difficult.

"Chad!"

Hair color was hidden by a cloth wrapping the head. Face was buried out of sight in the sand. Bare back was so brown it could have been Arab.

The distance to the body continued to deceive; the helicopter had dropped to give preferential access to the buzzard-eaten corpse, not the truck. Each step Ali took seemed to do nothing by way of narrowing the distance to his new objective.

When a buzzard beat Ali to his target, Ali feared the bird knew something he didn't.

Ali drew his pistol, aimed it, and fired. The bird exploded in a scatter of blue-black feathers.

Ali's legs were like lead weights. He came down hard on his knees besides the body. He reached for the makeshift *keffiyeh* and tugged at it. The material came free to expose Chad's blond hair.

Ali took hold and furiously shook his lover's limp body.

"Hi," Chad finally managed weakly. He tried to smile, but that was painful for his heavily chapped lips.

"Think I wouldn't make it?" Ali felt a rush of unadulterated exhilaration. He had fucking made it, just as he'd said he would!

"You did take your own sweet time." Chad let Ali help him to a sitting position. "Tell me you don't expect us to *walk* out of here."

"Come on." Ali hooked Chad's left arm around Ali's neck and helped the blond to his feet. "I've brought the carriage."

"The bomb is going to fit into that helicopter with us, is it?"

"There'll be others coming for the bomb." Ali would explain about the bomb being fake, later,

150

once Chad had recovered from the traumas of the past few days.

"And the Jew?" Chad asked.

Ali stopped their slow progress toward the pilot who was headed to give a hand.

"What Jew?"

"He wasn't a very talkative Jew, mind you," Chad said. "Probably because I disabled him with a bullet before suitable introductions. He's at the truck."

"Still alive?"

"I thought you might like to hear what he's doing out here, in the middle of nowhere."

"You're sure he's a Jew?"

"I'm, also, sure, surprisingly enough, that you, he and I, went to the same university together. Small world, isn't it?"

Ali thought Chad delirious.

"No kidding," Chad said once they reached the helicopter. "You'd better go get Alan Wayne, because he won't be walking anywhere on his own, the condition he's in."

"Move the helicopter closer to the truck," Ali instructed the pilot.

Alan was right where Chad said he would be, propped beneath the tarp awning on the flatbed. He looked more dead than alive.

"What in the hell are *you* doing out here?" Ali's question was rhetorical. Alan, his chest wrapped in bulky blood-soaked material, wasn't going to give any immediate reply.

Ali and the pilot lugged Alan into the copter and laid him out near Chad.

"Is he still alive?" Chad asked.

"Oh, I'm alive all right!"

Ali was surprised when Alan not only answered but miraculously conjured a Beretta M51 by way of follow-up.

"I told you, I wasn't going to die, you handsome son-of-a-bitch!" Alan informed Chad.

"I know what you *said*," Chad said. He, too, suddenly had a pistol drawn. "Are you alive enough, though, as you'll need to be for us to get done what we have to get done?"

Alan shot the pilot.

"What in the fuck?" Ali and Chad were now thoroughly, simultaneously, confused.

"Ali doesn't understand!" Alan said.

"*I* don't understand," Chad said. "Who's going to fly the helicopter?"

"I will," Alan said.

"You?" Chad was flabbergasted. "Even if you can fly it, what if you die at the controls?"

Ali heard but still had trouble understanding.

Alan aimed his gun directly at Ali.

"Out of the chopper, Arab boy."

How could Ali have gone so quickly from complete bliss to this?

"Out!" Alan repeated.

"I'll die out there without food or water."

"You'll die in here with a bullet in your heart, so your chances are better outside, especially when you'll be able to ride back to civilization with however many of your friends are incoming for the bomb."

Something told Ali that Alan and Chad knew very well there would be no one coming for the fake bomb.

(V)

ALAN TRIED TO TELL HIMSELF he had done right in killing the pilot. However, it became harder to convince himself that as he needed more and more concentration to stay conscious and keep the helicopter airborne.

What worried him was that he may have killed the pilot purely from some egotistical need to be more a part of the grand finale. If that were true, he had possibly endangered a finish more likely to have been successfully completed as Chad had originally conceived it. What happened if Alan let the copter crash?

Meanwhile, Chad tried not to think of how Alan could die too quickly; he watched the ground rise and fall beneath them.

Alan checked their direction. His teeth gritted as searing pain burned from his gut into his right arm.

Chad's attention turned on Alan as the helicopter tilted to correct their direction.

Alan's face was sweat-drenched. There were visible muscle spasms along his jaw line. His Adam's apple bobbed frequently as a result of reflexive dry swallows.

"You're going to crash us, aren't you?" Chad said matter-of-factly. "You're going to fucking ruin everything."

On seeming cue, the helicopter stopped all forward momentum and dropped earthward with a speed that brought Chad's belly into his throat. The descent aborted, abruptly, six short feet above the ground, paused momentarily, then dropped the rest of the way. The resulting jolt telescoped Chad's spine and chattered his teeth.

"Alan, you stupid shit!"

Alan wasn't hearing anything. He was slumped forward, his face pale, his eyes shut.

There was a sudden crackle of static over the radio, followed by a loud voice in Arabic.

(VI)

ALI BAHID FOUGHT HIS HOPELESSNESS.
There was no chance he would ever see Mahud Wadi again. Even making the attempt to cover the distance on foot, though desperation made him try, was pure madness.

He was unable to fit together all of the pieces that had brought Chad to take the side of the Jew, especially since Ali had proved himself loyal and a man of his word by coming back as promised. Not having the answers galled him. Not that knowing would change anything, but Chad's betrayal had played out too irrational to make any sense.

He stopped and stared at the apparition materialized in the sand just ahead of him.

The camel sensed Ali's presence and looked up briefly, then returned to eating from a small bunch of brown grass sprouting from the sand at its feet.

The animal was saddled, hung with leather accoutrements of various shapes and colors.

The absence of its rider left Ali thinking the beast merely a fantasy conjured by desert heat and Ali's fried brain.

The camel gave Ali another bored look and bared strong yellow teeth in a combination smile, spit, and snort. It began a slow amble in the opposite direction.

Ali followed, taking hope in remembering how the dead Arab found back at the truck site must have gotten into deep desert somehow.

CHAPTER THIRTY-ONE➔

(I)

CHAD SPENT THE REST OF THE DAY and most of the night positioned behind the M621 HMG heavy machine gun aimed out the side door of the helicopter. He knew nothing about the weapon, but he easily found its trigger mechanism and suspected he would have no more trouble mastering this gun than he had figuring out the Russian-made PPS43 during the attack on the convoy. Anyone approaching from the west would find Chad and the gun waiting. Anyone approaching from the east would, admittedly, have a better advantage. The gun's long barrel made it impossible to swivel it one-hundred-and-eighty degrees.

Not that Chad saw anything, either west through the open doorway or east through the small window that gave at least viewable access to that direction. However, Alan hadn't picked the most ideal spot for a crash-down from a defensive standpoint. Several large boulders and several sizable sandstone outcroppings offered suitable cover for anyone incoming and intend upon taking the helicopter and its occupants by surprise.

(II)

STATIC AND ARAB CONVERSATIONS continued over the radio and probably indicated that someone now knew Ali was missing. Although the darkness possibly assured no search parties would show until morning, the sun would undoubtedly bring a worried Riad Bahid out looking for his missing brother.

For the first time, Chad regretted Alan or he hadn't killed Ali when they had the opportunity. With Ali dead, and a dead Jew at the controls of the copter, Chad might have advantaged the viable lie that Alan had gotten the draw on Ali *and* on Chad. As things now stood, Ali was still alive to fill in the blanks.

Not that Alan *was* dead, yet, either. His pulse was weak, his breathing was shallow, but he was definitely still alive.

As if to verify that, Alan gave a low groan.

Chad gave one more check of the surrounding darkness. Seeing nothing, he moved into the cockpit to make another attempt at reviving the young Jew.

If they could just get the helicopter back into the air before the Arabs found them, there was still the slim chance they might accomplish exactly what Chad had planned.

(III)

WHILE CHAD'S LAST SPOT-CHECK hadn't showed him Ali, Ali had seen Chad.

Ali's camel had been left tethered in a concealing dry wash, its sides bellowing from its forced run.

Ali still didn't believe the twist of fate which had somehow allowed him, against all odds, to rendezvous with the helicopter, out here, in the middle of nowhere, Chad and the Jew hopefully none the wiser.

If he was confused as to why the helicopter had set down, still miles from the fortress, he wasn't about to tempt karma by too closely analyzing his stroke of obviously good luck.

There were, of course, a couple valid reasons that might explain the helicopter down. Chad and the Jew might have decided their move would best be accomplished under cover of deeper darkness, although the night was too far gone to support that theory. Maybe, the Jew's wound had forced them to land.

Whatever the reason, Ali intended to take full advantage of it, even if his only weapon was a Beretta M51 he'd picked up back at the truck.

(IV)

"SURPRISED?" ALAN ASKED.

"About as surprised as witnesses seeing Lazarus emerge from *his* grave," Chad confirmed

"I'm pleased your gentile upbringing hasn't left you entirely ignorant of *Bible* stories." Alan smiled weakly. He felt like hell.

"You Jews never had a monopoly on religion *or* circumcision." Chad wondered if he wasn't merely witnessing one final flicker before Alan's lights went out for good.

"Point taken." Alan licked his dry lips and hoped for a better mastering of his slurred speech.

"How do you feel?"

"Like warmed-over dog shit. I suppose you're anxious to continue our temporarily interrupted journey? How long have I been out, anyway?"

"Oh, only ten or so hours."

"You would think I'd be more refreshed after such a long nap."

"The radio has been making all sorts of noises. I couldn't make heads or tales."

"I would suspect it's merely reaction of our Arab friends' curiosity as to where Ali has gotten himself off to."

"Maybe you should call in and make some kind of excuse."

"Before I pass out again, you mean?"

"Before you drop dead, I mean."

Alan couldn't help smile.

Chad watched Alan work the radio controls. He listened to the brief conversation in Arabic that followed. He was fearful the other end couldn't help but notice the man on this end was obviously a Jew on his last legs.

"That should hold them for awhile." Alan breathed harder.

"What did you tell them?"

"That we had more difficulty in locating the truck than expected. That our radio is giving us trouble, or we would have checked in long before now. That we are headed back and will probably be with the dawn."

"They believed you?"

"They didn't have much time to ask questions. I told them our radio was fading, yet again."

"We'll never get there, now, you do know that?"

"That's meant to inspire me, is it?" Alan leaned forward and switched on the ignition.

In the darkness outside, the helicopter rotors began slowly to slice the cool night air.

(v)

WITH THE NOISE OF THE CHOPPER engine coming to life, Ali panicked. He wasn't, after all, immune to the irony which might have him within striking distance only to have the proverbial rug yanked right out from underneath him.

He was well into his slow approach from the rear but still had several yards to go.

Realizing he was suddenly in a now-or-never situation, he accepted the risk of exposure for a faster covering of the distance still left to go.

The helicopter began to rise before Ali reached it. It continued as Ali found an inner reserve to penetrate windy downdraft and jump one of the skids.

"Jesus!" Chad assumed the scary tilt resulted from either the machine's damage during its crash, or from Alan's continued state of near-death. Needless to say, he wasn't prepared for Alan's interpretation to the contrary.

"There's bloody something or someone out there!"

Chad made the effort to concur but saw nothing but one pod of the two for holding the four TOW missiles.

"I don't see a fucking thing!"

"Look again. Left skid."

The 9 mm Parabellum slug from Ali's Beretta ripped into Chad's suddenly visible shoulder (he'd been aiming at Chad's head), propelling the once leaning American back into the chopper in surprised shock. His head slammed hard against metal fuselage and left him all the more disoriented.

Ali moved quickly to utilize whatever advantage he had. He used a missile pod as a makeshift ladder to reach the chopper's still-open door.

He almost lost his grip before he succeeded.

He came up and over the lip of the available entrance only to be jettisoned into empty space by the force of the bullet Chad fired point-blank into him.

(VI)

RIAD BAHID STOOD ON THE BALCONY at Mahud Wadi. He gazed over the stone parapet for a first glimpse of his brother's helicopter incoming through the early-morning light. Another short-lived message had been received to verify its intended arrival

Ali had rescued his young lover, and Riad was now convinced of the necessity to severe all existing ties with his brother. Any additional association with a sibling so obviously ruled by his cock and balls, rather than by his head, would and could not bode well. Let Ali and his American ride off into the sunset and fuck their brains out while real and less emotional men involved themselves with the more important politics and power struggles of the real world.

He turned as Mifleh Zeid entered the room. The physicist was in charge of analyzing the real American a-bomb successfully air-lifted by helicopter to Mahud Wadi from Garuna shortly after the dummy bomb had headed off by convoy.

Not attractive under the best of circumstances, Mifleh's face was now twisted into even uglier contours.

"What?" Riad asked.

"The bomb may well be American-made, but it's definitely not World War II except in cosmetic construction that makes it look that way. What's more, its trigger mechanism is extremely sophisticated and complex as regards the apparently large amount of outside stimuli to which it's sensitive: close-proximity explosions, extreme heat variants, possibly even certain kinds of intense ground vibrations...."

"Fuck!" Riad interrupted.

Without even seeing the betraying flash of igniting missiles launched by Alan and Chad (the latter with a raging hard-on) from the helicopter just over the horizon, Riad knew, with intuitive certainty, what his infidel enemy had so-well orchestrated.

162

GENESIS 91:28➜

And he looked toward Sodom and Gomorrah, and toward all the land of the plain, and beheld, and, lo, the smoke of the country went up as the smoke of a furnace.

163

FINIS↓

www.ingramcontent.com/pod-product-compliance
Lightning Source LLC
Chambersburg PA
CBHW031605260626
47154CB00020B/1579